I0639027

INTRINSIC

Jerry Collins

Kwill Books

www.kwillbooks.com

I DEDICATE THIS BOOK TO ALL
THOSE WHO ENDURE TO
PRODUCTIVELY SUCCEED IN THEIR
PURSUIT, REGARDLESS OF
CIRCUMSTANCE, STATUS, OR CREED.

Table of Contents

"Many of us are caterpillars, but not all of us will reach our cocoon. A successful person doesn't try... they succeed." ~Jerry Collins

INTRODUCTION

In a world where nothing is as it seems comes a woman with the power to possess the souls and wills of men, to do with as she pleases. Jatara thirsts for world domination, moved by an unrelenting drive to capture and control the minds of her subjects.

This horrific saga of pain, betrayal and death takes place in ancient Europe, but the story transcends time, to the present and beyond. Jatara's plan for world conquest is only obstructed by Derideon, an omnipotent ruler of the underworld, who wants Jatara to join his regime and praise him as her master.

Will she obey? Or defy him?

The battle of wills has begun, but only one will thrive, and only the strong will survive.

CHAPTER 1

A man draped in a cloak tossed a torch into the barn that joined the guest and servants' cottages. He entered the main house and looted the library of books before setting the house ablaze. Afterwards, he released the livestock before they perished in the flames. This dastardly fiend committed robbery and murder, while the family dwelling within slumbered quietly through the night. A raging fire erupted, engulfing the house in minutes, leaving young Jatara and her family to die in a swirling inferno.

Jatara awoke to the sounds of agonized shrieks coming from her parents' room, followed by deafening cries for help. "Mama, Papa... where are you? I'm scared!" she wailed to the empty room.

As she opened the door and entered the hallway leading from her room, an enormous heat wave pushed her down the staircase. Jatara's small five-year-old frame rolled and tumbled to the front door. She pleaded once more for her loved ones to come out from that furnace of death. "Mama! Papa! Help me! It's hot and I can't breathe... Please, Papa! I'm scared!"

In that moment, the arsonist burst through the door, grabbed Jatara and carried her away from the house in the instants before it collapsed. "Come on, girl! You're no use to me dead! A heifer like you will make a great slave that will serve me well."

He dropped her on the ground and took off on foot before the villagers who had seen the flames had time to arrive. She shivered in the mud, wet and afraid, as feelings of despair and abandonment consumed her. Jatara was petrified, knowing that her loving family had just been destroyed.

She could see nothing but sorrow and vengeance in the future to come.

The approaching villagers would decide the orphan's fate. Egor and his companion, Zorka, the family's ex-servants, were the first to arrive.

They found Jatara on the ground and stood her up. Egor and his wife had accumulated a great deal of wealth working for the child's parents.

Egor was also the first parasite to initiate conversation. "Child, where are our masters? Have they been incinerated in that treacherous fire? Answer me, girl... what have you done? Were you playing with the oil lamp?" Jatara humbly submitted herself to Egor's inquisition, and tried to answer honestly.

"Lord Egor, I do not know what has happen to my mama and papa. I woke up to their screams."

"Did they make it out with you? How did you survive?"

"I didn't see them... someone pulled me out by the arm and dropped me in the road."

The village elders came forward to cast judgment regarding who would be assigned to care for Jatara. Jonas, the head elder, spoke to the crowd that had assembled in front of the smoldering cottage. "Jatara's parents are dead. They were ravished by the fire, which means that all their knowledge and protection that they gave to this village has gone up in smoke. Her father, Econ, and her mother, Shabella, provided our tribe with shelter against thousands of invading forces. Our crops flourished under their watch and supervision. If it weren't for them, we would be nothing. Econ and Shabella were our leaders... as well as masters of sorcery. The powers they bestowed upon us will never be seen again, nor forgotten in our lifetime. What will become of us is unknown; nevertheless, the truth must be told. Jatara, your family obliterated our enemies, and fed us with an abundance of nourishment. They saved our lives. Remember, child… life is what you make it, and the past is in the future. You come from greatness, and where you start is where you will return. Brethren, I fear that a scandal has occurred here. Whoever started this fire has sealed their doom."

Egor, standing amongst the crowd, relished the thought of silencing Jonas forever; he couldn't contain himself any longer. It was time for him to speak out. "I have potions that can enhance our crops. Why is it that you suspect foul play? What is the reason behind these accusatory statements that you continue to spew, suggesting that someone must have murdered Jatara's family? Anything is possible… the child could have knocked over an oil lamp. Lightning could've struck the house, or this simply could have been an accident!"

Jonas replied in an authoritative manner. "Egor, why is it that you have answers about an event that you know nothing about? Or rather, do you know about this event, and are now trying to cover your tracks? But where do they lead? Did someone help you assassinate Econ and Shabella? Why shouldn't I suspect you? If I really step back and look at your life, you have more motive than anyone to want them dead.

"You failed as a sorcerer and were ousted from their home for reading forbidden texts and stealing sorcery manuscripts from their library. You say you will protect us, but who will protect us from you and your sinister wife? Egor, you have said that Zorka will nourish us and replenish our crops. That is the same whore that Shabella found lying with your brother, Markal, on numerous occasions in the pigsty, roiling amongst dirt and dung. Your magic is mediocre and lacks passion. You will never be as powerful as the ones you took those powers from. Your spells were stolen, and not given, so they lack 'instruction. You operate on assumptions, devoid of knowledge. You question my relationship with this family?

"I was an apprentice and royal guard for Econ's father, who sacrificed his life force to save humanity. I was entrusted to protect Shabella and Econ, appointed by his distinguished family, who once ruled over Egypt, the Middle East and all of Africa. My life was entwined with theirs before you even existed. Do with me as you please. Egor, *lord* you are not. You aren't

3

worthy of that title. Only a traumatized child would call you that, for they lack the knowledge through desperation and fear. You are not fit to command this tribe."

Egor imploded, as the fury that had been building during the speech finally rolled over the edges. "Jonas, you accuse me of murder and the intent to commit treason. I should drop you where you stand! Your time shall expire soon; you are old and senile, full of lofty suspicions and paranoid delusions. I must lead through actions, not words. Jatara will live at my estate, until she is of age to entertain suitors. Child, do you object?" Her silence means no." Jatara offered minimum resistance, and said nothing. She knew that if Egor's request was denied, Jonas, her godfather, could be executed. Seeing her mouth remain shut, Egor continued, "Her silence shall be taken as a no."

Jonas interrupted, "My child, you can stay with me. I will protect you from this heathen." In a second, Egor was in front of Jonas. He knocked him down with a flurry of punches, drawing blood from his head, ears, nose, and mouth. Jatara, weeping, yelled out, "Lord Egor, please let him go. I want to serve you. Have mercy on him, master!" She pleaded for Jonas' life, knowing that if he died, Jatara would lose irreplaceable knowledge about her family's past and their royal lineages.

Egor articulated over Jonas' bloody and bruised body. "Old man, I will spare you this time. The girl has seen enough death for one day. However, if I ever feel that you deserve to be struck again, you will not see another dawn emerge on the horizon."

Jonas lifted his frail, battered frame off the ground, extending his hand out to Jatara. "Come here, child, your bravery has not gone unnoticed. Truly, I say to you, Jatara, true strength comes from within. Force is not always the solution to defeat one's adversary; nevertheless, being able to conquer someone's mind, and learning the ability to barter their soul for dominion over them... that is of greater precedence. Take my hand... see? You can feel the energy coursing through my being, but this is nothing compared to what your parents possessed. Your force shall be tenfold, far greater than Econ and Shabella. Egor may have damaged a three hundred and fifty-year-old body, but I felt no pain. Know that I had the strength and power

4

within my vessel to smite him and that harlot beside him. I could have eradicated both of them, ending their worthless marriage and existence.

"Instead, I chose to teach you a lesson. Sovereignty doesn't come from brute force, but through strategic execution of one's enemy through mental manipulation. The mind is the gateway to the soul. What I declare to you, no one else can understand. Only you and I, Jatara. It is the language of sorcery... called *kabar*. Jatara, you can already feel it. This power is in the core of your essence, this innate inheritance of discernment, just waiting for revitalization. You can bring this gift to life. It has been utilized for centuries within your expansive lineage of sorcerers and sorceresses. My journey is coming to an end, Jatara, but yours has just begun. The key to discovering the secrets of your ancestors lies within the books in Econ's library. These books will open your doors to unbridled power, along with unimaginable knowledge and endless life."

Zorka's patience had run out. She was tired of hearing Jonas drone on in a language that she could not comprehend. "Egor, silence this babbling fool. I want him out of the village. Cast him out into the wilderness. Let the vultures feed upon his decomposing flesh while he still breathes. This satchel of dust defamed my name. Show no mercy, my love. Eliminate him."

Egor began to approach Jonas again. "Old man, you speak incoherent riddles. You say words that mean nothing. Your tongue is loose and what I can decipher from your words is nothing more than arrogance. Jonas, you are henceforth banished from this village, and are never to return, doomed to live in exile for the rest of your days."

Jonas said nothing. He was prepared to die. He rose slowly to his feet and walked to the center of the town, to his home, to collect his belongings. He knew that there were people following him; he could hear rapid footsteps behind him. After entering his cottage, he peered out the shutters into an oasis of darkness, for the sun had yet to appear.

Have they sent mercenaries to end my life? he pondered for a brief moment. *They have come to kill the wrong man.*

No matter how dire that situation was, his reconciliation would be inflicting carnage with a vengeance, ravaging his assailants, which would give him some solace.

Jonas heard the men approaching the latched door. If they were going to act, the time was now. He spoke softly in *kabar*, with his arms extended forward and his fists clenched. A metamorphosis was taking place. As he ranted under his breath, Jonas began to change colors, turning from a brilliant orange to a fiery hue. The incantation ended, and he was Jonas no more.

His body was reincarnated into a lethal entity, bent on retribution, fueled with an insatiable desire to spill his enemies' life force. He unclenched his fists and a powerful burst of energy with the force of a hurricane struck the front door, disintegrating it into splintered projectiles, which struck four of the men in its path, leaving a bloody trail of destruction. They were swiftly exterminated, their bodies torn into hundreds of jagged pieces that landed on the remaining conspirators in front of the house.

Shrieks of terror rang out from the band of assassins. They could only hope that their demise would be as swift as the shredded men now littering the ground, and many immediately attempted to retreat.

From a few blocks away, Jatara had all but been forgotten, but she wondered what had happened to Jonas. *Was he okay? Why were people following him? What was all the yelling about?*

Her curiosity was overwhelming, so she climbed up a tree to see where everyone had dispersed. To her astonishment, she was witnessing a massacre. Jonas, or a fiery beast that looked like him, approached the crowd, and with surgical precision, he began opening their body cavities like pieces of candy, leaving a trail of organs scattered across the ground. His hands were instruments of death, hacking and tearing through men and anyone else foolish enough to contest him.

He pushed his arms through opponents' chests like a flaming sword through sheepskin, squeezing their hearts until they burst. A second surge of energy came from his hands once again, hitting six assailants, decapitating them instantaneously.

Jonas had been consumed by rage and thought blindly to himself, *"Their death will not be in vain, for I taught them well."*

Many of the attackers had been his own soldiers from the town's militia, which he had commanded for Econ. Jonas sarcastically reasoned that their foolish suicidal crusade was a sacrificial offering to Egor and Zorka, which he would gladly help them achieve, making certain that their blood would nourish the flies and their flesh would feed the wolves.

He methodically slayed his enemies, leaving them no chance of survival. The bloodbath continued across the village square; screams of pain and agony echoed from the dismembered fallen. Jatara viewed the devastation that Jonas inflicted with little emotion. She felt safe knowing that he was still alive, and acting as a force of retribution.

What she didn't know is that his survival would be short-lived. Jonas was deteriorating quickly.

Jatara climbed down the tree and ran towards him, knowing that he would keep her safe. Her honey-blonde hair shimmered as the sun rose above the horizon. The white tulips under her feet were covered with blood; body parts adorned the bushes and trees, where birds were already flocking to feast on the bounty.

She was elated to see him, and the thought of escaping with Jonas was overwhelming. "Jonas, let's leave here now! Please, take me away from this place. You're the only one who can protect me now."

He was touched by her declaration and began to reassure the frightened prodigy. "My child, you don't need my protection or help. Everything you need can be found within yourself. Just as I, a helpless old man, was able to transform into a vessel of vengeful anarchy, you shall also be transfigured when the time is right. Your powers will be unleashed on this world… there is no doubt about that.

"Jatara, it would be a honor for me to raise you, but that honor cannot be mine. I am dying, young one. I used the rest of my life force to vanquish those men, but that was a deadly choice. I knew the risk… either way I would die, and it is better to expire with honor. I chose to slaughter my enemies before

7

they slaughtered me." Jatara's eyes began to fill with tears, but before she could cry out, Jonas continued.

"Jatara, do not be sad about my passing. There is nothing you can do now. Listen to me. You have to develop mentally and physically in order to fend for yourself and become a great sorceress. After what I did here today, Egor and Zorka will fear you, and will certainly not try to harm you. However, his brother, Markal, is beyond reasoning... a monstrous psychopath. They have wronged you, and your parents, but that will be avenged later, in a world where you are judge, jury, and executioner. Your existence has been prophesied, Jatara, and foretold thousands of years ago. My child, don't be afraid... be courageous. You will live to see all those who rise against you fall at your feet. Remember, I was a servant of your grandparents.

"Unlike Egor, I excelled at casting spells and speaking in *kabar*. I became a part of your family. I've told you about your past, as well as your future to come. My loving debt has been rendered. I can now perish in peace. Jatara, the secrets of your gift lie within two books in your family's library. Be steadfast and unyielding when you are faced with difficulties... there will be many. Good fortune favors the brave."

After delivering his speech, Jonas dropped to his knees and his eyes rolled to the back of his head. Jatara's mouth dropped open as he began to dematerialize into a heap of gray powder that crumbled to dust. An unexpected gust of warm spring wind blew it away before she could comprehend what had happened.

Allowing the tears to roll down her face, Jatara walked away in shock, towards a creek near the village. She began looking for crayfish and frogs for dinner, something she had often done in the past. She gathered mushrooms, berries and wildflowers that she knew were safe to eat. This was something that she had done with her mother every day.

Sitting on the riverbank, she fashioned a crude spear to hunt wild rabbits and other small game. Jatara and her father used to hunt those creatures together. In an emotional daze, she foraged all morning, gathering a large stock of fruits, nuts, and vegetables.

Jatara wondered if Egor and Zorka would return to look for her, and whether succumbing to their capture would be wise. Could she survive without adults, especially those who were most likely responsible for her parents' death? Jatara began to think aloud, "I'm not able to live on my own right now, obviously. I also need the books that were stolen from my parents' home. I have no choice... I must go back to those who wish to control me, and gain the knowledge that will guide the rest of my life. I will recover what is mine, while building my strength to inflict pain on those who have taken so much from me."

Egor and Zorka had watched the entire scene from the safety of their house. They watched Jonas pass away and finally felt that it was safe to exit. Both were on edge, not knowing if Jatara had the same power as Jonas or her parents, or whether she had any idea how to control it.

Approaching Jatara as she re-entered the main square, Egor called out in a cowardly manner, "Jatara, are you harmed? Did that ogre hurt you? We came back to help you."

When Jatara didn't reply, Zorka spoke timidly, "My child, we'll feed you, clothe you, and keep you safe. I promise."

Jatara dropped the sack of food she had foraged and laid it before them. "I don't need you to eat, since I can light a fire, nor do I need you for clothing... I know how to weave. I'm only in need of shelter, so... I will stay with you."

Egor was infuriated at Jatara's disregard for the false gesture of hospitality. "You ungrateful little heathen... I should leave you to the bears and let the ravens feed on your carcass."

Jatara interrupted his tirade with a confident tone. "Egor, you should watch what you say and do to me. The same manna that Jonas possessed lies within me, only far greater. Do not provoke me. I can bring death upon you in a moment. My parents were burned alive tonight, and my lifelong guardian just disintegrated before my eyes. Do you understand what I'm saying to you? I am holding your life in my fingers, and my patience is nearly gone."

CHAPTER 2

Zorka, fearing for her life, pleaded with Egor to apologize. Egor needed no coaxing, however; his terror at Jatara's words was evident. "I meant no harm, child. I didn't mean to offend you. Please forgive me if I was too harsh in my words. I would like to provide shelter for you."

Zorka amended her husband's remarks. "Whatever we can do to help you, Jatara, just let us know. We would be honored to help you."

Jatara knew that her new guardians were afraid of her, which gave her a distinct advantage. Jatara responded with a tone of domination. "I will accept your offer to provide me with lodging, but no abuse of any kind will be tolerated from you or your husband."

Egor, feeling his anger rise at her tone, suddenly decided to challenge Jatara. He wanted to know whether she truly had the abilities she claimed. He ran towards her from a few paces away, taking her by surprise and pushing her to the ground. Jatara's head collided with a stone, knocking her unconscious.

Zorka was furious, but Egor grinned cruelly, disregarding the blood spilling from Jatara's head and ordering his subservient wife to carry Jatara into their home. After entering the abode, Egor motioned for Zorka to place the unmoving child into the cellar, and she locked the door to the room.

Zorka was elated to know that Jatara was no longer an immediate threat and announced her glee. "Egor, we are unstoppable! But my love, why did you let the girl live? She will rise up like an adder in the reeds and strike us dead. Jatara must die! Let me slit her throat. She may be as mighty as Jonas, or even more powerful than Econ and Shabella ever were."

Egor scorned Zorka, "Woman, you are a fool if you think I haven't considered that. Why do you think I attacked her? It was to test her inner strength and energy. Clearly, she has none. This girl will make a valuable slave or a concubine for a king if we keep her alive into adulthood. She will serve us until we sell her to another nation for gold or land. Be patient... we will profit from this endeavor."

Zorka was still intimidated by Jatara's presence, but she accepted Egor's judgment and questioned his decision no more. Egor instructed Zorka to let Jatara out of the cellar after she humbled herself and accepted her role as an underling. Zorka took the food that Jatara had acquired from her hunt and began preparing it for the three of them.

She thought to herself, *This child will make a good provider. I will have more time to spend with my husband and I will work her into the ground.* She smiled to herself as she chopped the wild onions.

Jatara regained consciousness on a damp cellar floor. Mice scampered past her head, but she could hear and smell food being prepared in the room beside her. "What happened to me?" she spoke aloud. "How did I get here? I must have been overtaken by Egor. Jonas was right... I'm not ready to defend myself... yet. I must gain more knowledge."

Jatara stood up with her fists clenched, shaking in anger, knowing that Egor had defeated her, for the moment. "I must obey their rules, but not forever."

She became compliant and submitted to her capture, realizing that she had no other choice. Jatara was famished and exhaustedly shouted from the behind the cellar door. "Please, give me something to eat. I'm hungry! I'll earn my meal, whatever you want me to do. I'm your servant and you are my master."

Jatara sat by the door, weeping in despair, for she knew that her life had forever changed. The security and love she had enjoyed with her parents in the past was gone forever. Jonas had told her to be patient and wait for the right moment to attack her enemies.

Jatara knew that her verbal assault had been ill advised. She needed more experience, which would take patience, and it was imperative that Jatara learned from her hazardous error.

Zorka heard the captive cry out for food and told Egor of her request. He immediately came to the cellar door and began to question Jatara's loyalty. "If I let you out and feed you, you must obey my every word. You will continue to hunt and forage, and in return, I will provide you with shelter from the dangerous beasts of the forest. Is that understood?"

"Yes, Lord Egor."

After hearing her conciliatory remark, he opened the door quickly, causing Jatara to inadvertently stumble forward. She slowly regained her balance, and was directed to a chair at the table, which was filled with food, mainly from what she had found during her expedition earlier that day.

Jatara began feasting upon the platters, stuffing her mouth with berries and pheasant meat, washing it down with warm goat's milk until her stomach was full. Jatara was constantly mindful of Egor and Zorka, who she caught looking at her intently. She knew that they wouldn't hesitate to attack, so she humbled herself in their presence, speaking meekly and with gratitude for what they had provided.

"Thank you, Lord Egor and Madame Zorka, for feeding me. I will earn every morsel bestowed upon me, and will serve you well as a loyal and obedient servant. I can clean and keep the house tidy. Lord Egor, I can also hunt and catch fresh game."

Egor and Zorka were impressed by Jatara's offer and her seemingly changed attitude. Taking this as the humility of the defeated, they obliged her request.

Zorka replied in a stern manner. "Jatara, do as you say and we will have mercy upon you, but if you disobey us, I will dispatch you like a mouse under a panther's paw. Dusk is approaching. Go outside and water the horses, clean the stall and bring in water from the well – three buckets' worth. Firewood is also needed, so get enough logs for tonight. Four bundles will do. After that, you can lay down for the night."

Jatara nodded and quietly set about the chores that were given to her, which took her hours to complete.

Jatara contemplated aloud as she worked. "Zorka knows that I'm a force to be wary of, and Egor's pride shall be his undoing. In time, they will forget about the danger I pose. My parents gave me the gift of infinite knowledge and kinetic power. Jonas knew this and so did I, even before he revealed it to me. Wisdom was bestowed upon me at the age of three, through a spell of enlightenment, which could only be performed by a master witch and wizard verse in the language of *kabar*. I happened to be the daughter of both. Why have I been given such an enormous responsibility as the sole caretaker of my family's wisdom and powers? Is it to contend with an even greater evil, or to punish all those who hurt me under the sole of my foot? I now lay upon a blanket covering straw, but it used to be silk spread on top of plush linen, fitted onto soft goose feather bedding. If these are the people who killed my parents, they will have their lives and souls torn from their worthless bodies. There will be no forgiveness on that day of retribution when I finally attack and kill my foes.

"Egor and Zorka's days are numbered. They will not know the day of their demise. I will strike like a mantis upon a blade of grass, impaling them with a deadly spear that they will never see. Everyone I love has been taken away from me. I have gone from playing with dolls to plotting the execution of my captors. I will avenge the death of my parents and find the true purpose of my existence. If I don't have a purpose, then I have every reason to die. I was not born to live and die without making a mark on this world. My name alone will cause rulers to fall to their knees and praise me. But first, I must unlock the mysteries within.

"To develop the energy within me, my mind and body must mature. I am still a child, and I know that wisdom without

13

experience accomplishes nothing. I can think no longer... I must get some rest. Another day awaits me." Jatara curled up on the bale of hay and fell asleep.

As the sun rose above the edge of the horizon, Jatara was awakened by Egor's call. He began listing the daily chores she had to complete, without exception, so she set out on another gathering and hunting mission. While picking wild strawberries and fruit, she feasted on some of the reward.

Jatara felt a sense of freedom and peace in the solitude of the forest. She reflected on many long walks she had taken with her parents under the canopy of lush green leaves branching out from elongated trees. Jatara yearned for Econ and Shabella's affection and their embracing arms.

Without that gentleness, she could already feel herself becoming rigid, and her thoughts were indecisive. "If I can hunt, then I can live on my own. The only reason for me to stay with those hideous cretins is finding those two books, which I desperately need. When I retrieve them, I will be a god – an unrelenting force to be revered, breaking the backs and necks of anyone who opposes me. I will tolerate nothing but total submission to my demands. Who I am is what I've become, and what I've become is a reflection of circumstances."

Jatara mused heavily on her situation and future ambitions for world conquest. As the morning progressed towards noon, Jatara hunted and brought down two hares, along with one huge wild turkey. On the way back to her prison – the cellar was no better than a cell – she noticed a man with a black cloak enter Egor and Zorka's house.

The sight of him sent chills down her spine. Was it the same man who had pulled her out of the fire and promised to enslave her? Why was he there? Had he joined forces with Egor and Zorka?

Jatara ducked behind a bush near the window to inspect the situation inside the house. The man in black dropped a large cloth sack on the floor, filled to the brim with books. Zorka was standing in front of him with a look of naked lust on her face; this was the man she had fantasized about for years.

"Markal, have you come to see my husband, or is this just an excuse to see me? Do you still think about our nights of pleasure while Egor slept? We would tangle together for hours on end... does it keep you awake at night? Your yearning for me?"

He responded with disgust. "You vile whore... why do you continue to dishonor my brother? The last copulation between us was devised by your trickery. We had decided that we would no longer disgrace Egor. Haven't you shamed him enough? I unwittingly ate the fruit from the shang berry tree, which you suggested, while I was watching and tending to his flock of sheep. Egor was on his monthly three-day militia duties at the guard post of your city. You offered this fruit, despite knowing the effects, which rendered me helpless and immobile.

"Instead of helping to rectify my condition, you decided to sleep with me, regardless of the fact that I couldn't stop you. The only good thing about that night is that I learned about the effects of this fruit. Your husband instructed me on how to use it against Jatara's parents when they were at their weakest – when they were asleep. I shot dozens of shang berry darts into them as they slept. Zorka, you only wanted to hide our indiscretions so you could keep coming back for more. However, I told Egor about your scandalous ways, and told him everything that had taken place between us." Zorka's face had twisted into a mask of rage, and she sputtered, unable to speak. Jatara watched from the window, shocked by all that she was hearing.

"Markal wanted me to earn his trust and forgiveness by disposing of Econ and Shabella, while retrieving all the books from their house. I have accomplished the mission required of me, but what have you done to regain his trust and respect? You can't even produce a child, let alone a son, you barren slut. Make yourself useful and let my brother know that I'm here, you worthless piece of bat dung. Go, get out of my sight before I slice open that lying throat with this blade."

Zorka scurried away to tell Egor of Markal's arrival. Upon hearing the news, he quickly came to claim his treasure. He was greatly pleased to see that his younger brother, who had fallen

15

so far from his grace, had now been vindicated. "Markal, you have certainly regained my trust. All is forgiven from this day forward. I also wish to reward you with a pound of gold coins."

Markal was astonished by Egor's generosity. "I appreciate your offer and will gladly accept it, but if I could exchange the ransom for the girl, that would be more to my liking. I could make a much greater profit on the slave market, considering her family's pedigree."

Egor was flabbergasted by Markal's ostentatious remark. "Jatara is not for sale, you fool. She is worth far more than a pound of gold. When you become a king, you can buy her for an appropriate price. Until then, she will remain with me.

Markal grimaced, but nodded his head. "I understand, Egor. Now, I must continue my journey while the sun is still up. This much gold is not safe to transport at night.

"Safe journey, Markal. Stay vigilant, brother. Farewell until we meet again." After Egor clapped him on the shoulder, Markal departed the house.

Jatara crouched deeper into the bush, glaring at the man who had just admitted to assassinating her family. She was mortified and vexed. Part of her wanted to leap out of the cover and attack, but to what end? The thought of vanquishing her enemies was tempting, but her inhibitions were important to maintain her safety. Her survival and ability to demolish her adversaries was dependent on her patience alone. Jatara wrathfully watched her parents' murderer walk away.

She found consolation at the thought of crucifying Markal, Egor and Zorka for what they had done. Death could not come soon enough for them.

Jatara regained her composure and gathered her belongings, including the animals she had hunted and the fruits she'd gathered that day, before entering the front door.

Before crossing the threshold, she took a deep breath and contemplated her situation. *"I must control my anger to survive this. The books that could free me from bondage and help me unlock my secrets have arrived. Oppression will not keep me from the knowledge within those books. My destiny was mapped out long before my arrival upon this earth, the prophecy of my eminent ascent will be fulfilled through those scriptures, and I will recover them in due time. My current circumstances are not a reflection of my future to come. This is only a mirage, a test of will that I must overcome.*

My parents bestowed great power upon me, including the gift of prophecy. Once I learn how to unleash this ability, I will be uncontainable... a force beyond reckoning. Anyone that stands against me shall fall beneath me, anyone that supports me shall stand beside me, and anyone who fears me shall serve me faithfully. I will serve and tolerate my enemies for now, but I swear to desecrate them later.

Unlike my captors, I will not strike under the shadows of night. What a cowardly cretin, to incapacitate such an exceptional sorcerer and sorceress while they peacefully slept, sending them into paralysis as they burned alive. These abominable monsters will know their annihilation is at hand when I rip them into chunks of flesh and pound their bodies into the ground. There is no reason for killing someone without purpose, but to slay my parents' killer is well within reason... Justice through revenge."

Jatara knocked on the front door before entering. "Who's there?"

"It's Jatara, Lord Egor."

"Come in, child... put down your load. You have served me well today. Zorka will prepare your food."

"Thank you, my lord, for having mercy. I appreciate your generosity, and I only wish to please you."

Zorka was infuriated by Jatara's total submission to her husband's demands; everyone was pleasing him except for her. Jatara's plan was working, which was to divide and conquer, causing any kind of opposition between the two of them. She knew of their existing strife and decided to use it to her own advantage. Relying on passive aggressive tactics, she could retaliate against her jailers without being in any real danger. Zorka was still fuming and it showed; her face was red as she stormed out of the house, slamming the door behind her.

Egor followed her in a rush, bewildered by Zorka's abrupt exit, and her blatant disrespect. He needed to reinstate his control in the household before anarchy ensued. "Have you gone mad, you foolish hag? Your emotions could cost us everything! You have already shamed me by sleeping with my brother, you unscrupulous whore! If you disrespect me in front

17

of this child again, or anyone else, I promise you won't live long enough to dishonor me again. Is that understood?" His eyes blazed, and she knew not to challenge him.

"Yes, my lord, I will abide by your rule. What you say, I will do," she replied humbly.

"Then go back inside and prepare supper. Make yourself worthy of my presence. If you can't serve me, then you are of no value to me." Jatara was busy preparing and cleaning the game she had caught when Zorka and Egor returned.

Egor was surprised to see that, despite her option to have her meal cooked by his wife, the child would still be diligently working. He was genuinely impressed by her effort. Egor ordered Zorka to take over and instructed Jatara to rest until the food was prepared.

Jatara showed her appreciation for his sentimental offer and accepted it graciously. She knew that gaining Egor's trust would lessen his strict control that kept her in the home, eventually allowing her to access the books of knowledge and sorcery. The thought of discovering and reading about her family's past and their powers bolstered her motivation to continue her facade.

Jatara closed the door and laid down on her straw pallet, thinking of ways to further manipulate her captors. *I have driven a wedge between Egor and Zorka, but I must continue this endeavor. I need to take advantage of the divide between them. I need to exploit this division and find my time to study those books of enlightenment. When I turn six years old tomorrow, it will not be a day of celebration.*

Despite that reality, another day alive gives me another day to devise a plan to eliminate my parents' killers, and those who have turned my life into a nightmare. My age does not represent my wisdom, nor does it blind my ability to see my value to Egor, as well as his fiendish scheme to exploit me. I know everything that has happened to my parents, and I long for the day when I will avenge their death.

I am a product of my parents' love and their lives will not have been taken in vain. I was born into a peaceful existence, but that life is gone. I shall bring a flaming sword of retribution upon those who have wronged me, breaking the backs of those who have oppressed or hurt the ones I love. Tomorrow is another day closer to my destiny, and for that, I am grateful.

My birth means nothing, but the legacy I leave behind will leave an everlasting footprint upon the Earth...

With these grand thoughts swimming through her head, she closed her eyes and allowed dreams to come.

CHAPTER 3

The aroma of food ascended into the room and pulled her back into wakefulness. She was starving, and was looking forward to feasting on the delicacies that she had gathered.

Zorka called Egor to the table to eat and then summoned Jatara to take part in the banquet. Egor told Jatara to fix her plate and she eagerly complied, running to the cauldron, scooping out the rabbit and pheasant stew into a large bowl, and quenching her thirst with freshly crushed berries drizzled with honey, which she poured into a hefty cup from a pitcher on the counter.

She sat down and consumed her food feverishly. Jatara was famished, given that she hadn't eaten since the day before, and had used every scrap of energy from that meal. Egor and Zorka ate until their stomachs were content, and then offered Jatara what was left. She happily accepted it and gorged until she could eat no more.

After finishing her meal, Zorka ordered Jatara to clean up the kitchen and then return to her room. She added a final remark with reluctance, "Lord Egor has requested that you work in the house tomorrow. He will advise you of your chores in the morning. After you're done washing the dishes, return to

20

the cellar and don't come out unless you are told to. If you do, I will go back to locking the door. Remember, girl, you may have Egor fooled, but he is fickle. I will gladly slit your throat and watch your blood trickle out slowly. I don't like you, so you had better stay in that room... just give me a reason to send your ass to hell."

Jatara replied in a deep, brutal tone. "Zorka, I guarantee that you don't know me at all. If you approach me like this again, I'll cast a spell. You think you're strong, but to me you look frail. I tolerate you, for now, but those days are numbered. If you threaten me again, your life will fall apart. Leave me alone or burn in hell." Zorka fled without saying a word, frightened by Jatara's powerfully authoritative tongue.

She decided that night to avoid confronting the child unless it was absolutely necessary. Zorka didn't mention what had happened to Egor, knowing that she had already slighted him earlier that day. Zorka was petrified of Jatara, and that emotion couldn't be controlled any longer.

At night, her thoughts ran wild: *Is that girl truly capable of destroying me? I wouldn't be surprised... how is she capable of hunting, preparing game, and speaking like an adult at only six years of age. This child has power unknown to me... beyond anything Egor understands.*

Zorka scurried to her room, got into bed, and lay trembling at the memory of Jatara's voice as she floated in and out of consciousness.

Meanwhile, Jatara was thinking about what had transpired between her and Zorka. She felt that there had been no choice but to defend herself. The delicate recollection of standing up to that lustful monster enthralled her. She knew that one day soon, that dastardly trio would be desecrated by her hand. Jatara envisioned them being slowly decapitated and disemboweled as she drifted off into a tranquil sleep.

As the night progressed, she dreamt deeply, and had recollections of how her loving parents would embrace her many times throughout the day, particularly over the last two years, teaching her the earliest elements of sorcery to enhance her innate abilities and powers, and even giving her lessons in the language of *kabar*. That advanced language of sorcery, used

21

and developed by her ancestors to cast incredible spells, was always a pleasure to hear spoken. Jatara's parents had truly given her abilities far beyond her years.

The sun began to rise as Jatara girl woke from a peaceful sleep. She was ready to take on the day, regardless of what challenges it might bring forth. Jatara got up and began making a big pot of porridge and skillet bread, with a scent that billowed throughout the house. Egor stumbled into the kitchen and was stunned to see Jatara up so early, already preparing breakfast. Although he was perplexed by this, Egor was appreciative of a hot meal in the morning.

"Jatara, you have pleased my palate. I'm glad that you have become a good servant. For that reason, I will allow you to work inside today. Zorka and I will hunt and gather today while you clean the house. I want it to be tidy in every room, except the storage room. You are not to enter that room. If you continue to follow my instructions, your tenure here will progressively get better. One day, you will clean the living quarters, and the proceeding day, you will hunt for food." Egor sat down and motioned for Jatara bring him what she had cooked, along with a cup of crushed berries.

After fixing his plate, she was asked to join him, but Jatara declined, stating that she wanted to be sure Zorka would have enough to eat. At that moment, Zorka entered the kitchen and rejected the offer of breakfast, claiming that she didn't feel well, and walked out. At that point, Jatara shrugged, retrieved a plate and took Egor up on his offer. They both ate every morsel of porridge and skillet bread. They didn't speak.

Upon finishing their meal, both rose and went about their new routine for the day. Egor packed his hunting gear and headed out the door, where Zorka was already waiting. Before leaving the premises, he repeated the chore list for Jatara, again mentioning her strict avoidance of the storage room, and then disappeared with his wife into the woods. Jatara was ecstatic; she had the house to herself for the first time, which meant a chance to look for the books that could liberate her.

Jatara cleaned every room top to bottom, but initially bypassed the storage room. *What could be in there?* she thought.

For an hour or so, she avoided thinking about the room, but the temptation was overwhelming. *If only I knew how long they would be gone...* Even so, she knew that she was going to enter the forbidden room. It was a risk worth taking. Her life was nothing more than a series of gambles, interspersed with rage and deception.

Egor's acquisition of Jatara and his demand of unwavering obedience to him was horrible, not to mention his early attempt to intimidate her with physical harm. In her mind, she had nothing to lose. Jatara slowly crept towards the restricted door on her hands and knees, completely quiet and totally alert. She needed to get in and out without being detected.

As she entered the room, she felt a sense of serenity taking over, as if she had returned to familiar ground, so she began to search the room with an oil lamp. It didn't take her long to find the source of her calmness, like a beacon of light in front of her, guiding the lost child to salvation.

Jatara walked towards the two large sacks sitting near the wall, as though a magnetic force were drawing her near. She was compelled to open the sacks, and to her astonishment, the books from her family's archives lay inside. History that extended over a millennium was contained in that collection of manuscripts.

She reached for a book and immediately felt a shock of energy surge through her body. The text was foreign, but understandable, as she could decipher *kabar*, giving her a tremendous advantage over her captors. She leafed through the book, where every page included notes and handwritten instructions about Econ and Shabella's potions, which they had developed depending on various needs over the centuries. The next book was focused on spell casting, and explained when, where, how and why certain spells could be formulated.

Jatara began to feel uneasy, not knowing exactly when Egor and Zorka would arrive, so she decided to cease her research, for the time being, and took both books into her room and concealed them for further investigation at a later date. Moments after exiting the cellar, the front door was flung open. Zorka and Egor came bustling in, dragging a large deer and a

23

small basket of wild strawberries they had picked in the forest. Jatara's parents had created gardens for everyone's home in the village, but when they died, so did their gardens.

Egor pulled the feet of the buck to the back porch where he began gutting and chopping the beast into more manageable pieces. Zorka collected every chunk of meat and hung them in the smokehouse to be dried and preserved. Egor called for Jatara to assist him in collecting the cured meat that was hanging there from previous ventures, and placed it in a barrel with salt to be stored for the winter months.

Jatara had to focus hard on the task at hand, as she was still energized by her discovery, and this was not the time to rejoice. The true undertaking was to build up the abilities given to her by her parents, to utilize the tools and knowledge in the book and learn how to eventually destroy her enemies. She salted the meat methodically, putting every piece in a different section of the barrel. Jatara longed for the day to end so she could begin her studies.

Egor observed her unusual mannerisms, quick and almost impatient. "Child, is there something bothering you? You seem preoccupied... what's troubling you?"

"Nothing my lord. I just want to do my best. I was concerned that I hadn't cleaned the house properly. You never mentioned what you thought of my work." Jatara had not known that her inner thoughts were surfacing, and scolded herself. She would have to keep her emotions in check to maintain her secrets.

Egor was satisfied with her response and fell silent, turning back to his work. Zorka, on the other hand, was waiting in the wings, darkly hoping for a clash between Jatara and Egor that would result in the girl's death. Alas, this was not the moment.

Zorka announced to the pair that the table had been set. Jatara knew that Zorka detested her and that Egor was just using her, but nonetheless, for a brief second, she felt a connection, as though Egor and Zorka had become a family.

However, she also knew that these people were responsible for her ultimate sorrow, as well as the death of her parents, either directly or indirectly. Their punishment would come, and it would be savage, regardless of how they treated her until then. Jatara refused to relent, and thought of little else but eventually vindicating her fallen parents.

The sun was beginning to set over the horizon and it was nearly time to settle in for the night. She was ready to begin her studies on the books she had obtained. As Egor and Zorka headed to their room for the night, they turned off the oil lamps in the hallway and retreated inside. When their door closed with finality, Jatara leaped into action, retrieving an oil lamp from the kitchen and pulling both books out from under her pallet to begin reading. The first book she grabbed said *Volume 1* on the binding, and she assumed it was as good a place as any.

The first chapter explained how Econ and Shabella had met over three thousand years ago, as servants working on the pyramids of Egypt. The text also described how they had used their powers to influence pharaohs, allowing them to control the people who resided on the lands they conquered. Jatara now understood why she had such an insatiable desire to conquer and control; it was clearly in her blood. She was more fascinated by each subsequent passage; each page spoke of an event when a different potion or spell had been used to accomplish a particular goal.

The next four chapters described how their powers had been enhanced by a voodoo priest deep in the Congolese jungles. Econ had been a student under the tutelage of that priest for two hundred years, just as his father had done before him. All master sorcerers followed this path, and over those generations, he and his clan controlled most of Africa. Eventually, Econ made his way to Egypt, where he infiltrated the power structure under the guise of a servant. He wanted to learn the ancient magic that elite spell casters used, such as other master sorcerers in his family who had learned here. It had been foretold by his father, Kragon, that the source of enhancing one's power was within the borders of Egypt.

It was there that he met Shabella, who had come from Greece, his very first homeland. Econ spoke of sailing from Athens two hundred years earlier in search of medical herbs to save his ailing father, one of the master sorcerers who had sacrificed their life force to trap Derideon underground.

Two hundred years later, he was nearly immortal, a living god; all that had needed was to obtain and secure the spells from the dead shamans, which lay within the tombs of the mummies. This information, along with all he had learned from the voodoo priest, would make him invincible. Shabella became Econ's protégé, friend and lover; he taught her everything that he knew, including powerful spells and potions. Together, they were a formidable and ambitious force.

Jatara continued to read hungrily through the passages, and learned that her father had been nearly four thousand years old, and that her mother had been five hundred years his junior. She knew that their abilities had extended their lives, but she had never suspected they were so ancient.

After conquering one dynasty after another, collecting immense amounts of wealth and knowledge along the way, Econ and Shabella chose to settle down and have a child in their native land of Greece. First, they had to fortify the new nation they were creating in Spain, which was under siege by an unknown force.

The book described legions of fighters who brandished fangs and rode huge wild horses, tearing the heads and limbs from anyone they encountered. Their agenda was unknown; they asked for no bounty or food. It seemed that these savages were only concerned with death, torture and mayhem, which they inflicted with gleeful malice on the populace, regardless of age, gender, or surrender.

Econ had to bring an end to this league of killers, and the army he assembled was composed of highly skilled mercenaries who had fought with him before and overthrown many legendary kingdoms. Now, his warriors would be put to the ultimate test.

Shabella rode into battle with her mate, refusing to be left out of the fight. Econ cast a spell of protection on his troops, a thousand men strong, and also enhanced their strength with a potion of fortitude he had concocted. Unfortunately, this didn't prepare them for the slaughter to come.

The carnage took place on an open plain. Econ and Shabella, along with their soldiers, arrived as another massacre was taking place in one of their provincial villages. Approaching the city's entrance, they witnessed the men, women, elderly and young of the village being torn apart by these demon warriors. His men could hardly tolerate the sight; they had seen enough innocent blood being shed. They unsheathed their weapons and charged toward the insurgents, wielding their swords with precision, attacking the mass of murders with a singular purpose.

These men were highly skilled, but that was irrelevant. Their rivals were horrific monstrosities, moving so fast and violently that the soldiers' efforts were in vain. Every time they slashed, the deranged beasts dashed out of reach. Econ was astonished at how swift these demons could move, effortlessly evading the blades of his men. Even when they made contact with great hacking sweeps, it didn't seem to affect the monsters in any way.

When the beasts retaliated, however, the results were sickening, and they quickly tore through much of Econ's elite army. The legion of killers appeared undefeatable, readily severing the arms, legs and heads of their opponents bare-handed, leaving a trail of torn flesh behind them, their ghastly claws dripping red from the carnage.

Econ and Shabella knew that they had to act quickly, before they were all destroyed. The pair began speaking in *kabar*, conjuring powerful spells to eliminate their resilient foes, which took far more effort than they initially realized. The first spell slowed the beast's to less than half their normal speed, giving his soldiers a chance to escape their deadly grip and land key blows.

The beasts quickly shook off the spell, however, and the next assault they unleashed on his men was tremendous, leaving even more mangled bodies strewn across the land. As the army retreated, Econ and Shabella combined their powers and life forces to create a shield around the remaining citizens and soldiers, allowing them to flee the scene. Econ lost more than half his force in a matter of minutes, and was becoming increasingly concerned for Shabella's safety... they had never faced such a formidable force. Nevertheless, he needed her help to end this atrocity.

The blood lustful fiends were four hundred strong, and were still advancing towards them. It was a desperate moment, so Econ made a desperate request. He asked Shabella to release her life force to him, promising to revive her once the battle was over.

She hesitated for only a moment, but trusted him implicitly. After she passed her life force over, Econ, freshly filled with unimaginable power, carried her unconscious body deeper into the shielded area, where his soldiers carried her the rest of the way to safety, placing her on a guarded cot near the center of the shielded space – the most well defended area.

Econ then fell into a trance, and appeared to flicked in and out of sight, before descending beneath the earth. The ground around the invaders turned from a green turf to smoldering coals, spitting incinerating flames between the vicious beasts. The horses on which they rode fell and exploded, melting into lumps of scorched flesh, while hundreds of the foreign invaders were similarly devoured by flames.

Econ's attack wasn't completely successful; some survived by climbing over the charred bodies of their fallen comrades, proceeding ever closer to the protective shield where the remaining survivors huddled, hoping that Econ would be successful in thwarting the last of these apocalyptic murders from breaching their final line of defense.

The demonic mob ventured closer, beginning to stalk and charge the crowd. Fortunately, they couldn't penetrate the shield, and were thrown back several yards after touching the edge. Undeterred, they persistently continued, slashing at the barrier, weakening its ability to keep them out.

Econ stepped back outside the shield to extinguish the last of the hideous minions, neither man nor beast, alive or dead, possibly some type of demon.

Econ wondered who could have sent such a devastating force to slow his advance into Europe. *Who would dare oppose me, and have the ability to launch this type of savagery against my land and people?* He confidently stepped towards the invaders beating the edge of the enclosure. His arms transformed into blades and his hands became flaming torches. He leaped into the center of the lurching, foul beasts, executing them mercilessly, slicing and burning their flesh even as they disintegrated.

His eyes were full of fire as he approached the last fiend standing, who he began to question. "How did you get here? Who sent you? Who is your master?"

The demon smirked and answered mockingly. "Econ, you fool… you ask how I arrived and who sent me, but those queries are beyond your understanding. Your ownership of this land is an illusion. It always has been. My father sent us to remind you that everything you have is thanks to him. The power you wield is not yours, but borrowed by my creator, Derideon."

Econ was agitated by the words, but responded boldly. "Derideon is nothing without a host, and I do not serve him, nor will I ever. I have vanquished many empires under his rule, and brought down many men who bellowed his name as they took their last breath. Your father is damned to lie locked beneath the earth, but I do not. Why should I worship something I cannot see? Derideon attempts to win my allegiance by spilling the blood of my men, but it is futile. I will never succumb to his rule. I am my own master. He will not decide my fate."

Derideon's minion rolled his eyes, but they showed a sliver of fear. No need to kill the messenger."

Econ sarcastically replied, "Why not? You deserve to die. This is my gift to you… your head rolling in the dirt, your entrails burning as they are swept away by the wind."

Econ kept his promise and a second later, he swiftly beheaded and incinerated the evil creature.

Jatara had begun to fall asleep after reading the fight scene in the sixth chapter, and decided to turn in for the night, already eager to read more tomorrow.

She hid the book and returned the oil lamp to the kitchen before lying down in the cellar for a deep, dreamless sleep.

CHAPTER 4

Morning had arrived and Jatara was still asleep. She was awakened by Zorka cooking breakfast for Egor, and was ordered to get up and set the table if she wanted to eat. Jatara complied, prepared the table, and fixed Egor and Zorka's plates.

Although she felt exhausted, the stories from last night filled her with energy. She could hardly believe that her parents had endured so many life-threatening challenges and prevailed to become important leaders. They had forged a path of defiance and nonconformity in the midst of tyranny and evil.

Jatara's resolve for justice was strengthened by what she had discovered, giving her a heightened sense of pride and stoicism to make it through the day. There was an abundance of deer meat left, so there was no need to go on another hunt. Instead, Egor told Jatara to cultivate the garden and prepare it for seeding; only a few patches of fruits and vegetables had survived after Econ and Shabella's murder.

Jatara used this opportunity to test some of her newfound skills, creating a simple potion she had learned from the book to enhance the flavor, quantity and size of the fruits and vegetables over the course of two weeks. After the garden chores were completed, Jatara was free to do as she pleased. Egor and Zorka had no further chores for her.

She thought about all that she had learned and was overwhelmed with excitement, so she began recanting spells in the woods, quietly speaking *kabar* to the beasts and birds. Jatara's abilities and manna were increasing with every recitation, and she could feel the warm glow of magic within her chest.

Jatara was still tired from the previous night, so she sat down beneath a tree and slumbered until it was time to eat. Even her dreams revolved around studying the books; they had consumed her life overnight.

Unbeknownst to Jatara, Egor and Zorka had been discussing how Jatara's attitude had changed, which worried Zorka. Egor, however, saw it as Jatara becoming more familiar with her surroundings, meaning that she was comfortable and had accepted her fate as their servant.

Zorka was not convinced. She didn't trust Jatara and let Egor know of her concerns. "My lord and husband, this girl must be watched closely. She is more than meets the eye… her mind is deceptive, just like her parents. She is not innocent, nor has she ever been. I… I fear what she is capable of doing. I just don't want you to be deceived, my love. Watch her closely, Econ. Assume nothing. To trust without prudence can be deadly."

Egor took heed of Zorka's plea, but replied with a pacifying diatribe. "Zorka, I will be more attentive to Jatara's evasive ways; I haven't turned a blind eye to her. I see through what she does, which is how you examine a person's motives. We are defined by our actions, not our words. Don't worry yourself over childish concerns, my love; she is just a child. I will sell her to the highest bidder when she reaches the age of sixteen. The girl shall fetch a huge return; she is the daughter of Econ and Shabella, two of the most indomitable sorcerers to ever walk this earth. Kings and queens will come on their knees from all sides to claim her royal lineage. We will be rich beyond our loftiest dreams. The books alone are priceless, containing immeasurable knowledge. They could turn a wizard into a deity. That is why we must tolerate Jatara; she isn't worth anything

31

dead, beaten or bruised, neither mentally nor physically. She is an investment that must be preserved."

A few miles away, Jatara awoke to a large black bear standing above her, sniffing her arms and legs, but the beast soon passed by, seeing that she wasn't a threat or a potential meal. She was startled, given that she was a small child up against a six hundred-pound beast. Jatara rose and headed back to her residence, and began to contemplate… *Tomorrow, I will cast a protection spell over me, so that when I'm asleep, I will be safe. I wish my parents had done that on the night they were killed. How could they have known that those who lived in their own village had such murderous intent, all for the sake of thievery and wealth.*

Jatara vowed to never make the same mistake as her beloved parents. Entrusting her life and safety to the horrors of mankind was a foolish thing to do; she vowed to always remain vigilant. On her walk home, she noticed that something had been following her. It dashed from tree to tree, scampering along behind her, instantaneously disappearing when she cast a glance over her shoulder. It traveled too fast to be seen or to discern what it was. She was curious, but not afraid; if her parents could defeat a legion of demons, one mysterious beast shouldn't be too much for her. She clenched her fists and readied herself for an attack that never came.

To her surprise, moments later, a young squirrel appeared, clearly playing a game of hide-and-seek with her. She laughed hard, despite the tears coming to her eyes. The interaction tickled her, as her parents had always called her squirrel when they played that game with her.

Egor and Zorka were waiting outside near the front door with their steeds saddled. "Child, where have you been? I was worried about you. Don't wander so deep in the forest… it's dangerous. I was just on my way to search for you when I saw you emerging from the woods."

"My lord, I didn't mean to concern you. I grew tired while exploring, and laid down to rest under the shade of a tree. I dozed off and slept for hours. Please, forgive me if I have troubled you in any way."

Egor, Zorka and Jatara went back inside together and ate dinner in near silence. Shortly after the adults finished their meal, they retreated to their room, leaving Jatara to complete the kitchen chores. An hour later, she crept back to the cellar and closed the door, eager to resume her studies. The oil lamp was already lit, as she had been given permission by her benefactors to have a light in the room. She flipped open the pages and found the place where she had left off...

The warfare with Derideon's forces would change Econ and Shabella's lives forever, namely by impeding their campaign of world domination. Econ and Shabella returned to Greece and reasserted their rule over that region and much of Europe.

They reigned over the continent for a thousand years before settling down to create a family. Eventually, Shabella became pregnant with Jatara. Econ was thrilled have a baby after two and a half millennia of dominating and eliminating his opponents. He was ready to be a father, to have someone to care for that was a part of himself – an innocent and precious life uncorrupted by sin. Econ longed to hold his child. It was an incredibly new experience, but one that he relished.

Although these first-time parents were thousands of years old, you couldn't tell by their appearance. In fact, they didn't look a month over twenty-five. Econ had spells and potions for everything, including youth enhancement and age regression. In order to be completely devoted and doting parents, Econ and Shabella relinquished their control of Europe and appointed successors to rule in their absence. The appointed leaders shared the couple's passion and ideas for governing of the citizens, along with keeping them safe from invasions.

All the leaders were selected generals from Econ's army – loyal delegates who would lay down their lives for him... people who he could trust with his empire. After securing their dynasty, it was time to retreat from the global eye with his wife.

Econ and Shabella thought that those they appointed would remain loyal, but after the couple was killed, their façade of loyalty crumbled, and they never checked on Jatara's welfare. Luckily, her godfather, Jonas, had stayed true to the family and

33

kept his word to Econ and Shabella to protect and direct their daughter, even to his dying breath.

Jatara continued reading, scouring every page as fast as she could, and then returning to savor the seemingly important parts. Econ desperately wanted to be a good husband and father by supporting Shabella through the struggles of her pregnancy.

Zorka had actually been one of the midwives, administering help and comfort to Shabella during labor. Egor, an aspiring sorcerer and Econ's student, claimed to possess the gift of sorcery. He was taught and tutored by Econ for six years, but never developed into a viable sorcerer and ultimately failed at his endeavor.

Egor wasn't taught the tongue of *kabar,* a language reserved for master sorcerers. In the wrong hands or an unskilled student, *kabar* could be a disastrous weapon, capable of inflicting carnage upon oneself and others. Econ was highly selective of those to whom he taught this language. Shabella was the first and only person to whom he taught *kabar.*

During the last three months of Shabella's pregnancy, many preparations had been made for the child's arrival. Much of the work was joyfully done by Econ, who built a crib, playpen and nursery for the baby's arrival. Neither Econ nor Shabella cared if the child was a girl or boy; they just wanted a baby of their own to hold and love, someone to inherit all their wisdom and sorcery, a vessel of knowledge in the form of a child…

Jatara stopped reading after the tenth chapter, flipping back through the book to refresh herself on the previous chapters before going to sleep. She dutifully wrote down a short list of spells to cast and potions to formulate during her next excursion in the woods.

As the sun rose, Jatara was already outside, watching it from the front porch, gazing at the top of the tree line. She began reciting a spell of enhancement, which would give her the ability to harness nature's gifts for her own benefit.

She spoke quietly in *kabar* and began shaking wildly, her clenched hands turning a fiery red. Jatara rose off her feet, moving towards the sun, where she became a brilliant reddish-orange silhouette. The spell worked and her confidence soared as she landed back on the ground. Her hands opened and an immense burst of energy and heat flew from her grasp, colliding with a tree and disintegrating it instantly, leaving a heap of ash piled in the grass.

Jatara spoke in *kabar* again, to release the power of the sun from her body. It traveled from her chest, down to her arms, and out from her hands, streaking into the sky. It was an amazing sight – a pillar of flames blazing across the clouds, bending towards the sun until it disappeared into the stratosphere.

*

Jatara developed her craft in solitude, and she spent the next three years obeying and acting the part of a dutiful servant, while honing her powers to a razor's edge. She was now nine years of age, and Egor had accepted her into the family, considering her trustworthy and completely harmless to them.

Zorka eventually developed a fondness for Jatara, particularly when they hunted and did chores together. Jatara hid her manipulative connection and her ulterior motives well. She also continued to advance in her training, mastering the techniques of spell casting and potion mixing that she acquired from the books, without Egor and Zorka ever knowing of her nighttime lessons. She was still adamant about enacting revenge on those who had wronged her, and was reminded of that hatred every day.

Jatara was waiting for the right time, and as she grew older, her mind matured and became less impulsive. Jatara used her powerful aptitude to make life more convenient, bringing down large game animals with ease and finishing work around the property swiftly.

However, these activities were becoming mundane; using her massive talent for such trivial purposes was irritating. Jatara was eager to start her life as conqueror, taking back her parent's legacy and reclaiming their domination over the world.

On one particular day, Egor walked into the house looking for Jatara, bearing a gift for her from a wealthy prince of a kingdom near their village.

The inhabitants of the village had been reduced to ten families, primarily due to the battle between Jonas and Egor's assassins – men from the village. After their death, the surviving women and children had left to find suitors to help raise their families.

Jatara was not impressed with the offering from the prince. She had received many presents from kings and princes over the last three years, each wanting to gain Egor and Zorka's favor in order to take possession of Jatara at a later date, once she had come of age.

Egor received many lucrative offers and bribes for her, but he refused them all. He knew that she would be worth much more in a few years. Furthermore, all the gifts that she received acted as an endless source of valuables; he sold many of the treasures and kept the coin for himself.

Egor approached her with the prize and began to speak of its beauty. "Jatara, this gold and platinum sword is magnificent. Your presence is requested. His offering has pleased me beyond words. Men have come far and wide to bid on you, but I want only the best for you. When you turn sixteen, I will match you with the wealthiest and most astute ruler in the land. You will live as a royal servant, a dignitary, princess or even a queen for some mighty dictator! That all depends on who wins your hand. Although you have grown up in the last few years, you must still be cautious when traveling in the forest by yourself. There are many dangers lurking there. I rarely see you during the day… most of your time is spent in the woods. Why do you avoid Zorka and I, even though we have tried to treat you well? I am truly concerned about your wellbeing… what is ailing you, child?"

Jatara was flabbergasted at the parasite standing before her, pretending as if he cared for her. She knew that it was all an act to win or retain her approval, which Egor felt was slipping away.

Jatara went on the offensive, retorting with condemnation. "Egor, you say that your heart is with me, but I think you mean that your heart belongs to the profit you will make from my exploitation. Don't act as though you care for me or my life… I know better. I am nothing but currency to you and Zorka. I can accept this, but I can't accept you blatantly trying to deceive me. If you told the truth about your nefarious plot to auction me off, and fatten your purse, that would be compassionate and display your integrity to the one you oppress. Yet, all the gifts I receive you take and barter for your own profit. If you want me to be cordial around potential suitors, don't continue to lie. I am not a fool, nor do I intend to be treated as one."

Egor was at a loss for words, and not knowing how to respond frustrated him. "Child, how dare you speak to me like that, after all I have done for you! I gave you food, protection, shelter… and this is the gratitude I get? You ungrateful heathen," he spat angrily, his eyes flaring. "I would thrash you to death if your life wasn't worth so much. That is a fact you should never forget, you little orphaned wench. I am your lord, and you shall obey me! I give you what I want you to have, not what you want me to give you. You deserve nothing."

Egor stomped away, irritated, realizing that his scheme was transparent; all his deceptions were unraveling.

Jatara did not allow him to walk away; she followed closely behind, and he whipped back around at the sound of her voice. "Am I supposed to fear you? You're nothing but a spineless maggot. I could end your life in seconds. I have only tolerated you all these years to build my strength. I have developed more than you can comprehend. I chose to dwell here… I was not your captive. But now, my powers have grown beyond my need for you. You are an imbecile to think that I would not possess my parents' power. I have been studying their magic for the past three years. Yes, I taught myself, and I had excellent motivation – avenging my parents' death." Jatara's eyes flashed menacingly and Egor could barely speak, let alone move. "I've read all the books that you took from Econ and Shabella. I'm so much stronger and wiser than I was that night, and my resolve hasn't wavered. Not once. I still plan to end the lives of my parents' killers. Yes, you. Why did you and your brother murder my family, Egor? Was it all for greed? Or did you hope to unlock the secrets of their magic by stealing these books? You must ask yourself, why would I possibly spare your life? The answer is simple… I won't. You will die. Along with Markal and Zorka. There is no other way that this story ends."

By this point, Egor was shaking with anger and apprehension, not knowing whether she was telling the truth, or if his life was about to end. "Please, child, don't push me to punishing you. I will not allow you to contest my authority. Have you gone mad? Are you saying these things for attention? Why are you threatening my life? Can you even follow through with your threats? Or are you stupidly claiming to be something you're not? This isn't child's play, and I won't treat you like one. Nor will I spare your life in battle. I demolish my foes, and you won't be an exception. Pick your side, child… you're either with me or against me. If you're the latter, I will kill you where you stand."

"Egor, I don't fear you or your clan. When I choose, I will kill you in front of the tribe, the village and any visiting kings or princes that happen to be visiting, emptying their coffers into your pockets. I could end your life right now, but that would be too easy. I will make a spectacle of your deaths, I promise you… fetch your wife and brother so they can die with you."

Egor was furious, but also terrified. He could not tell whether this was bravado, or the end of his reign. He stumbled from the house towards Zorka, who was coming in from the garden. He began to explain what had just occurred between him and Jatara, but as he spoke, Zorka's eyes trailed back to the cottage, where Jatara was levitating and glowing a brilliant fiery orange.

In a deep, confident tone, she challenged Egor to a duel at dusk in the town square. Both of her captors were speechless, and she clenched her fists as she floated past Egor and Zorka, glowing angrily as she entered the woods.

Jatara was no longer willing to live behind the facade of a helpless, victimized child; her physical appearance didn't match her mental prowess, but after that night, she would be known as a ruthless conqueror. As Jatara moved deeper into the forest, Egor and Zorka jumped on their horses and rode for their lives, finally realizing how wrong they had been. They came upon Markal exiting his home and told him of their plight. Egor told Markal and Zorka that they had to battle Jatara in the town square or lose everything, including their status, wealth and lives, not to mention their claim on Jatara, allowing them to sell her into servitude.

Egor spoke solemnly and dramatically, attempting to rally his army of two to fight valiantly. "Your courage must not falter. This child must be stopped by any means, even if we have to poison her with a shang berry. The right amount will sedate her, and too much will kill her, but it's a chance worth taking. We can dip some darts in shang berry juice and shoot her in the neck or back at the right moment. If we do nothing, she will destroy us all. Jatara's ambition to defeat us during the parade of suitors this month must be suppressed."

Markal was hesitant, shaking his head and speaking out against their futile mission. He wanted nothing to do with the ordeal. "I say we count our losses and leave while we're still able and alive. She is clearly dangerous. Based on your account, she can levitate, which means that she likely has the potential to cast spells. I want no part of this; even if we are able to sedate her, what happens after the effects wear off? We don't stand a chance against the powers she may control. We are ants under the foot of an elephant.

"Our resistance is useless, and I choose not to be obliterated. You can meet your death with an ignorant hope of survival, but I will not. I'm going to escape now, before it's too late. When the storm hits, there will be nowhere to run or hide, and you're charging right into the heart of it. Egor, your plan has failed. You never deciphered the manuscripts of Econ and Shabella, and your powers are no greater than they were three years ago! Don't forget that I am responsible for their death, but you and your wife are conspirators. However, I refuse to die by a child's hand."

Zorka was deflated, feeling her life crumbling to ash in her hands. She had nothing to say and remained silent. Instead of agreeing to stand by Egor's side, she fled with Markal to dodge Jatara's deadly, vengeful rampage. She had foreseen this years earlier, despite Jatara's apparent domestication. The trio, with heads hanging low, sped through the forest, leaving the village forever.

However, their escape was stopped by an incredible surge of wind, a tornado directed by the furious hand of a god that violently swept them up, whipping them above the tree line, crossing miles in mere minutes. Zorka's screams were blood chilling.

The stunned conspirators were thrown like discarded trash in the middle of the town square, where they tried to rise to their feet, failing to notice the visiting king and prince from the neighboring wealthy kingdom, who were already assembled. Legs had been broken, faces were bloodied, and Zorka's moans of pain were incessant.

Jatara had met with the king and prince earlier that day and had prepared a lavish meal to honor these dignitaries. However, to exemplify that she was not going to be a servant, but rather a conquering sovereign ruler, she dropped her parents' killers at their feet and offered the visiting rulers a public execution.

The king, prince and accompanying guardsman were astonished by what was transpiring before them. Jatara's hands began to glow, and a terrible smile spread across her face at the horror in the faces of her parents' killers. The violence was incredibly intense. Egor, Zorka and Markal were once again picked up by the carefully wielded twister and then hurled viciously to the ground, where the sound of bones crunching on the earth caused shivers to race up every spine.

CHAPTER 5

The trio attempted to rise to their feet, trembling and dazed, knowing that death was imminent. They tried to escape, but they had been crippled, and cried out in agony at the smallest attempt to walk.

Jatara swooped upon them like a falcon on its prey. She grabbed Egor, who began to beg for his life, while Zorka and Markal stood by, mortified and unable to move. They could only hope for a swift and certain death.

"Jatara, my dear merciful child, I raised you into a young lady and you repay me with death? I gave you food, shelter and protection… and in return, I receive betrayal? You were an orphaned child who I exalted to the ranks of a royal servant. I gave you the chance to be a princess or a queen! Please… you don't have to kill me. I did nothing to warrant this execution. Should I not get a trial, and be judged before a jury? Or have you assigned yourself judge, jury and executioner?" Egor was desperate, knowing he only had moments to live.

Jatara snickered cruelly as she replied. "No, I will not spare you, just as you did not spare my parents. Econ and Shabella were your masters, and entrusted you with their lives. No, I will not kill you while you sleep, as you did to my beloved family. I will destroy you here, in front of the villagers, and our visiting guests. Your passing will not be quick or merciful, Egor. You will beg me to finish your life. You are a candle in a blizzard, easily eradicated. You are like a stillborn child… your life has meant nothing, and your begging is nothing more than frivolous banter. It makes your cowardly existence an even greater pleasure to extinguish."

Jatara began to glow, which grew to a fiery blaze that encompassed her entire body. Without another word, she proceeded to brutally remove his appendages; her hands became daggers, cutting through his flesh like a machete through an ear of corn, severing his arms first.

Egor screamed, shrieked and moaned in agony, still pleading for his miserable life as blood spurted and gushed from his wounds, showering the cobbled ground. His detached arms and legs fell into a blood-soaked pile beneath his torso.

Tendons and muscle tissue dangled from his shoulders, spurting out his life, while his lower stubs began to slow their outpouring of blood. His cries for mercy were ignored, as she casually ripped out his tongue and gouged out his eyes.

With her fist tightly closed, Jatara smashed it through Egor's chest and tore out his heart, reveling in the few beats it gave off in her hand. His body thudded to the ground limp, broken and lifeless.

Without pause, Jatara menacingly walked toward Markal, who was cowered in a state of shock at the massacre of his brother at the hands of a child. She forcefully grabbed his arm with the grip of a gorilla, splintering his bones like icicles, dropping him to his knees.

Jatara then reached down and removed his leg, rending the femur from the flesh, as a beastly cry tore from his lips. The dripping heart from his brother's chest still in hand, she smashed it down his throat, breaking his teeth and choking him to death.

Jatara rose back into the air and commenced to smash Zorka across the head with Markal's leg bone. A shrill eruption of pain burst from her lungs as her skull split in half, sending blood and brain matter cascading into her lap. Before she realized that she was dead, she twitched and tumbled to one side, never to move again.

Jatara took a deep breath and then turned to those in attendance, who were silent, mortified by what they had seen. None wanted to be her next victim.

With blood spattered in an angry pattern across her face, she addressed the crowd of villagers and guests. "For those who don't know me, I am Jatara, daughter of the omnipotent masters of sorcery, Econ and Shabella. My parents were slain by these three fiends, and now, justice has been done. For those who have come here to bid or buy me, know this… I will never serve or be suppressed by anyone. Today, I have liberated myself from my oppressors, and do not seek another. My destiny is to conquer the kingdoms of the world, and that conquest will begin here. All who wish to join my regime may peacefully submit to my rule, or face my wrath." Jatara gestured to the gory scene at her feet, accentuating her point. "You also can return to your kingdoms and tell them of what you have seen. Some of you may try to defeat me, but you will fail. I was destined to rule this nation and many others. You can support me now or be conquered later. I leave the choice to you."

Her speech done, whispers began to carry through the crowd. Many of the onlookers joined Jatara on the spot, pledging their unwavering allegiance to her quest for world domination. Seeing the tide begin to turn in the favor of this demonic child, the rest of the assembled villagers and guests agreed. Exhausted, but overjoyed by the destruction of her greatest enemies, Jatara retreated to her home, cast protection spells on the entrances, and fell into a deep sleep.

Under cover of darkness, those who promised to join her army fled in terror, never to return, leaving the ten-year-old child to once again fend for herself. She was left without any guardians, free to do as she pleased.

When she awoke, there was no one in sight, as they had all abandoned her. Momentarily surprised, she vowed to never again give her subjects the option to serve or not. Only total subordination would be accepted.

Jatara decided to use the time provided by this recent desertion of sworn servants to hone and perfect her skills even further, tapping once more into the knowledge of her ancestors. Weeks of study turned into months, which grew into years, and she was becoming a terrifying force. During those years, she also amassed a substantial military force of peasants and refugees, with whom she would ride into engagement with on her eighteenth birthday. Jatara was completely prepared to subjugate the world.

Her name alone was enough to evoke hysteria and panic in bordering kingdoms and distant empires. Her reputation had preceded her, and she was widely known to not only be a master practitioner of sorcery, but also a vengeful, pitiless killer.

She passed those same hateful traits onto her army, while also giving some of them endowments of enormous proportions. At the tender age of sixteen, an invading collaboration of tribes, numbering five thousand, tried to overtake Jatara's newly formed troop of one thousand, who easily vanquished their foe, leaving only one man standing to speak of the macabre events he observed. Because of the destruction of those invaders, their lands were now a kingdom that she ruled, and the terrified occupants praised her name. Jatara was now powerful enough to overthrow any kingdom she wished, including the one she had petitioned that fateful day in the town square, when she avenged her parents in bloody fashion.

Having offered him peace the first time, she didn't ask the king to surrender the second time around; instead, Jatara went directly to the head of state and decapitated it, pulling those lands into her own, claiming every resource and creating another kingdom for herself.

The defending nation had been heavily fortified, with a stone wall standing thirty feet high, with archers positioned every few meters on the battlements, eagerly waiting to send a hail of arrows into the heart of any opposition. They also had a cavalry of five thousand men who were ready to ride at moment's notice, along with an infantry of six thousand, half of whom were mercenaries ready to earn their pay.

King Rasupeus had even commissioned rogue sorcerers to help disband Jatara and her intruding marauders. He vividly remembered the display of her lethal power against her enemies years ago at the celebration of suitors. He managed to organize these defenses against her army, but he feared it wouldn't be enough. Jatara and her men, who exceeded three thousand cavalry and two thousand infantry by that time, rode towards the wall, where they were showered with arrows. Her shield of protection deflected every arrow within its range, flinging them back to their bows, and through the chest of the archers, tossing hundreds of bodies off the wall within minutes. Most were dead before they hit the ground.

The second onslaught from the legions of King Rasupeus was just as desperate as the first. Their cavalry was relentless, and within minutes, hundreds of mortal wounds were struck on each side. A select few of Jatara's elite forces of infantry and cavalry took to the air, hovering over the king's horsemen and ground troops, attacking them from above, removing heads and slitting throats, thanks to Jatara's enhancement spells cast during the battle.

These elite fighters were a band of eight hundred highly skilled warriors who had passed the rigorous selection and testing stages under Jatara's tutelage. They received the honor and prestige to join this exclusive echelon of fighters, and were then specially trained to absorb and utilize her tremendous energy when it was bestowed on them.

Although her army suffered some losses, far more would have perished if Jatara's elite warriors had not fought beside them. They were messengers of death, darting back and forth, executing countless cavalry and infantry rivals. Jatara lost fifteen hundred men, but not a single elite soldier was killed. King Rasupeus' outcome was far more dismal, losing six thousand men, the vast majority of his forces.

Those who survived the initial massacre pleaded for mercy, laying down their weapons and joining the civilian population, hoping that their lives would be saved. Jatara allowed them to live, as her qualm wasn't with the army. However, the man who had assembled the army – the king of their nation – was

45

retreating further into the bowels of the fortress. She knew that with his head on a pike, the battle would be over, and she would easily be able to conquer the kingdom.

As she entered the iron gate of the fortress, none were brave or insane enough to oppose her. King Rasupeus was holed up in his royal tower, along with his servants, son and concubines. He furiously ordered his sorcerers to protect him from Jatara's wrath, but they wisely refused and fled. They hoped to avoid detection by Jatara and her elite warriors, who were making their way towards the king's last line of defense.

Deserting sorcerers slithered out of the tower, right into the grasp of the approaching army, which detained them, demanding the location of king Rasupeus. The cowardly wizards divulged this information without the need for coercion. They were even willing to lead Jatara and her men directly to the king and his family.

Jatara spoke boldly to the sorcerers, curious about their training and power. "Who was your teacher? You all clearly lack integrity, loyalty, honor and valor… why should I let any of you live?

One tall, dark-skinned man stood up and faced Jatara. "I am Kalan, the leader of this faction. We know that we couldn't compete with your immense power and invincible army, so we humbly surrendered. We all come from different nations, and learned under different teachers, but none were your equal. If you allow us to live, we will pave the way for your arrival in other lands. We will tell our leaders what transpired here, informing them of your strength in both war and sorcery. I am certain that they will wisely offer no resistance to your demands."

Jatara nodded, clearly pleased. She had been convinced by Kalan's speech and decided to spare their lives. She proceeded to the massive tower, her private cadre of elite soldiers behind her, as she made her way up the winding steps.

Upon entering the room, she found king Rasupeus on bended knee, worshipping a statue made in her image. This greatly impressed Jatara, who appreciated the likeness on the stone. She stood six feet tall with curly honey-blonde hair hanging to her shoulders, silhouetting her shapely frame.

"Rise, Rasupeus. Given your show of homage, I will permit you and your family to live. You will watch over my kingdom, and command your citizens to worship me. I have spared their lives in exchange for their souls, which is the source of my power. If my power declines, I will know that they are not praising me properly. I will execute ten people per day until it increases. Warn them of this. Know this, Rasupeus… if you betray me, I will destroy you and your family without hesitation. After delivering her declaration, she left the tower, eager to enjoy the bounty that this newly acquired kingdom had to offer.

*

Jatara and her soldiers ate, drank and danced for weeks, which stretched into months and years, before they set out to conquer another nation. Upon their departure, Jatara, who was now twenty and beloved by her kingdom's occupants, was showered with gifts and food rations by her subjects; it would be a long and tumultuous journey to the next kingdom. Many men and soldiers from the conquered kingdom had joined her army, which was now seven thousand strong. She also kept some soldiers behind to protect her new sovereignty.

The next kingdom she sought to conquer was very strange, situated both in trees and underground, making it hard to attack, as there was no real point of origin. The enemy forces were scattered everywhere, swinging in trees and running beneath the ground, and were legendarily difficult to fight.

Jatara wondered briefly if they were worth dominating, as they had almost nothing of material value. They lived in trees and dressed in leaves, lacking any structures to signify ownership or the power of their nation. However, their landmass was a bridge between eastern and western Europe, so it was a necessary route if she wished to continue her inexorable march to other viable nations. Jatara had even heard peculiar stories of cannibalism within the kingdom, which she observed during scouting missions to the area.

She had been intrigued by what she'd seen – a group of tree-dwellers armed with swords, consisting of men and women with sacks and rope tied around their waist. She witnessed them climbing out of the trees by way of wooden pegs inserted down the of side of the bark. Once they passed the web of branches, they leaped horizontally between the trunks, dropping lower and lower, constantly monitoring the ground below.

As their feet touched the soil, they attentively surveyed their surroundings and sought out livestock to plunder. You could distinctly hear the loud creak and rustling from underfoot. None of the ground dwellers were in sight, as they had descended into their underground lairs. The tree dwellers entered livestock pens in this way, making it nearly impossible to see their approach, grabbing chickens and pigs, while another group plundered the gardens. When their theft was done, they tugged on the ropes and were lifted back to safety, but many didn't make the return ascent. The ground crumbled at various locations, due to traps set by ground dwellers, causing these scavengers to fall on large stakes, which impaled them.

Small fires burned around the stake to roast these tormented souls. Those who died instantly were lucky, although this rarely occurred, and the few who survived and resisted the ground-dwellers' demands died a hideous death. They were pulled off the stakes, despite being severely wounded, and then thrown to the wild dogs chained around the circumference of the pits. The hounds would rip them to pieces and consume their flesh until only the skulls remained.

Jatara witnessed a particularly brutal scavenging party, where thirty tree-dwellers went down, but only seven came back. Most who returned had food in their sacks. Some carried vegetables, and others brought livestock, which they shoveled into huts constructed out of tree branches and lumber. Within these trees, the loot would be divided amongst the community.

They would return to the ground as a group once every month, but between those large hunts, one member per day would venture to their almost certain death.

Jatara and a unit of two thousand soldiers marched into the heart of the peculiar realm, but she left the remaining forces slightly behind to rest and prepare for battle, just in case she needed them. She erected a shield of protection to hinder an onslaught of attacks, which could emerge from below or above.

As she and her troops entered the territory, a frail tree-dweller with dark red skin and a rope tied around his waist was lowered onto a branch thirty feet above them. Although above their heads, he was directly in the path of their progression, and began spitting sneering questions at Jatara. "Why are you here? Are you going to destroy us? Your reputation spreads abroad, and we know that you are a great conquer. However, we have already been conquered by a force far greater than you. He is ancient and very powerful. He rules the underworld, but will soon rise above into this world. Do you serve him? Are you a slave to Derideon?"

Jatara was infuriated by the mindless stream of questions, but kept her composure. "I serve no man or demon, nor do I serve a ruler who hides in the mud and slides in the shadows of trees. I am Jatara, and my name delivers fire upon my enemies. My presence will shatter any kingdom that fights my control. I am the new ruler of the earth, above and below. I know of Derideon, as did my predecessors. I am not impressed by one who rules through a demonic vessel, stripping his slaves of free will. He is a demon enslaver who is damned to live underground, and is therefore no threat to me. Are you one of his minions, tree-dweller?"

"No, Jatara, I am a victim of his minions. My people are hunted and sacrificed to give Derideon the strength he needs to rise up and dwell above the surface. The ground-dwellers are his servants; they butcher, eat and torture us until we swear over our souls to their leader. Then, we are converted into Demon knights or ground-dwellers. The woods are littered with death pits. If you or your army pass through here, they will surely perish. Are you our liberator, Jatara? Or a new slaver? Who will save us from these vicious demons? You?"

"How did this happen? What happened here? I cannot help you if I don't know how you became ensnared in this deadly trap." Jatara softened, genuinely interested in the dynamics in this strange kingdom.

"Ten years ago, a strange man came to our nation and demanded that we worship his master. We refused and he began slaughtering our people, including our king and queen. He laid waste to our once magnificent kingdom, which had been bustling and thriving with over seventy thousand citizens. It was swallowed up by the earth and buried below the ground. One demon knight and an army of one thousand, each with the fortitude of a hundred men, with powers never witnessed by those who survived. Some of us fought, but many of us surrendered and gave praise to Derideon.

"Upon submitting, their souls were taken, and they became remorseless zombies, dedicated only to causing death and destruction to please their ruler. Those who refused to worship Derideon fled to the trees, where the ground-dwellers were unable to reach us, but our numbers are diminishing. When we first entered the trees, there were three thousand of us who survived the conversion, but now, only two hundred of us are left.

"Our livestock and gardens are tended to by the ground dwellers, who attempt to lure us from the trees into their ghastly traps. Many of us have fallen. We have archers who are told to kill our captured brethren, before they can be taken over by these demons. What must we do to receive your mercy, Jatara? Please, I beg of you… deliver us from this hell and we will serve you well.

"You are certainly worthy of my deliverance. Any people that can fight and survive this long, facing almost certain death just to eat, deserve to be in my army. I admire those tribe members who have survived; you have shown incredible perseverance and an unyielding nature. Your people have endured much, but for my protection, you must worship me and surrender your soul, as all my soldiers have.

"That is how I can protect you, by channeling your souls into energy, which I can turn against my enemies – and yours – to destroy them. I can also harness the sun and all of nature's other celestial elements. So, yes… I will free you from these shackles of death, which have imprisoned you for all these years. Your enemies will become mine, and they will suffer a fiery demise. If you want to live, bow your heads and praise me. You will become a part of my glory; your energy will help to defeat the nations that oppose us. We don't take prisoners, the conquered either assimilate or are destroyed."

The tree-dweller looked wary of such an offer, but he also saw no other hope for his people. He shrugged his shoulders and closed his eyes. Jatara smiled at the sight, and shivered. "I can already feel your energy coursing through my veins. Now that you have agreed to my terms, I can make good on my promise. Stay in the trees until the smoke clears. Then, you can reclaim your forest."

Jatara and her squadron crept deep into the woods, levitating past countless death pits and traps, approaching the spot where the ground-dwellers were located. They were eventually confronted by a group of mindless, zombie-like minions under Derideon's control; they spoke in unison, using the language of *kabar*.

The sound of her magical language was very disturbing to Jatara, but her elite warriors and regular forces were more disturbed by the appearance of the slaves, who were grossly mutilated and disfigured, yet somehow, they still lived... and looked ready for a fight.

CHAPTER 6

She contemplated how this could be; only under Derideon's command could these damned souls exist. Jatara used this strange encounter to unify her army. "All of you must remember what you have seen here, to inform your brethren of the devastating consequences that Derideon inflicts on his servants. When you serve me, you still possess your mind and will. You're conscious of your actions.

"I only use your souls to enhance my life force, strengthening my power. In return, I can allocate the energy back to you when you need it most, making you effective weapons of destruction and war. These grisly abominations are mindless drones that speak only the mind of their master. We will listen to Derideon's messengers in order to understand his method of deception. You can't defeat your enemy, unless you understand his reason for deceiving you.

One of the zombies under Derideon's control turned to the recently arrived forces and approached. Jatara bristled, but did not attack, waiting for the beast to speak. The zombie's mouth moved, but the words were clearly not his own.

"Jatara, join me. I have a place for you in my army if you submit your soul to me. I've been observing you for quite some time. You have matured into an instrument of calamity, causing death and mayhem as you tread across the earth. I admire your ambition, but nevertheless, you cannot possess the world alone. It takes collaboration with a deity, such as I, to direct and protect you from the forces that seek to destroy you. Jatara, you cannot succeed without my assistance. If you don't join my regime, you will surely perish.

"The power you possess comes from me, but you don't acknowledge me in any of your conquests. This must end today... here and now. Jatara, you must pay homage to me. All the souls you control are to be released into my possession. Your army will become my army, and your soul will become my soul, to control with my wisdom and expertise. Bow down and praise my name. I tell you this, just as I told Econ and Shebella. Serve me and become immortal... defy me and die." Derideon's slave ceased to speak, waiting for Jatara's response with an unblinking gaze.

"Serve you and become immortal, but I will only be an immortal slave. I think not. You have nothing to offer me or my soldiers, unless it's a mindless life of servitude. You ask me to condemn my people to a life of illness, mental desolation and destruction of the flesh, but we would rather die. Derideon, how can you call yourself a deity when you govern through zombies and battle with brainless corpses? You are not deity. You are nothing but a coward hiding under the shadows of fleas. I fear you as I fear a light mist carried by an ocean breeze.

"You are of no consequence to me, nor do you intimidate me. I will never join you. My parents didn't succumb to your demands, and neither will I. Derideon, you can send your pathetic minions to challenge my elite troop, but they stand no chance. My soldiers fight by choice, as well as for the personal gain of treasure and bounty. The fighters you command are lifeless vessels, fighting for reasons they cannot comprehend. They have no purpose and are bound to fail. I know why you want to acquire my essence; with me, you could rule above the ground once again, becoming an unstoppable force capable of destroying humans forever. Derideon, I am not your savior or liberator, and you will not succeed with my assistance. The one thing I will do for you is send you and your servants back to the

53

depths of perdition. I may not be able to kill you, concealed so far beneath the earth, but I will send your soldiers to join you shortly, destroyed in a blaze of fire, unable to serve you ever again."

The air surged with powerful wind, as though the forest was preparing for war. A great battle was about to ensue. Jatara summoned her troops from the outskirts of the forest, a force of five thousand heavily armed men, combined with the elite force that had accompanied her into the woods. The tree-dwellers watched in astonishment, amazed that anyone or anything would dare to oppose Derideon and his soldiers, who had massacred and terrorized them for years. The tree-dwellers watched with a mixture of joy and fear, for they knew that if Jatara failed, they would be the next target for Derideon and his zombies' unbridled rage.

Jatara began speaking in *kabar*, her eyes rolling back into her head. The sky darkened and electrified bolts slashed in and out of the clouds, striking the innumerable enemy forces emerging from underground, disintegrating some and dismembering others. Jatara's shield of protection covered her troops and allowed them to hover over the trenches that had been dug by the ground-dwellers.

Her army's elite forces led the charge, bearing flaming swords, burning and slicing through enemy troops. Jatara fought alongside the elite force, running into battle with a fierce cry of rage, engaging and eliminating her adversaries with countless lightning bolts, striking them savagely, severing their soulless bodies into chunks of smoldering flesh, laying waste to everything in her wake.

As the battle raged on, Jatara's army incurred substantial losses. The shield couldn't hold forever, as she needed much of her power to cast spell and enhance her elite forces against the seemingly never-ending army of demon knights, all of whom were larger and stronger than the ground-dwellers.

The ground-dwellers and demon knights proved to be ferocious; they used battle-axes and long ghastly claws to chop, tear, rip and bite into her soldiers. In addition to the deadly pits where the wild dogs, which had been unchained, snarling and sundering flesh on all sides.

By the end of this gruesome battle, Jatara had lost half of her elite force, and an even larger amount of the regular force. However, all Derideon's ground-dwellers had been killed, and the cadre of Demon knights had been reduced to a manageable few.

Derideon, sensing that defeat was imminent, brought the knights back below ground. A loud rumbling sound came from the earth, followed by a voice denouncing her victory and swearing to enact revenge upon Jatara and her army.

The ground began to shake and tremble violently, causing some of the tree-dwellers to lose their footing and tumble to the ground, fortuitously landing on dead soldiers, which broke their fall.

Derideon began speaking once again from beneath the surface, echoing across the land like thunder. "Jatara, you will suffer untold pain for your defiance. My power is suppressed now, but that is only because I am confined. Above this earthly prison, I was exponentially stronger than you and your family put together. I was one of the most powerful forces to ever inhabit this realm. You know nothing of me, only what you read from your parents' library. That is only what they wanted people to know of me.

"I have existed for countless millennia as an unharnessed force, but that was before your ancestors confined me below the earth seven thousand years ago. It took three millennia and more than two hundred master sorcerers to confine me in this subterranean tomb. Your family studied my power for thousands of years as my apprentices, and then used that knowledge against me. Does that sound familiar? Isn't that how your parents met their demise? Ah, yes... now you are wondering if I had something to do with Econ and Shabella's death? Of course, you foolish child. I sent a demon to poison the mind of Egor, Zorka and Markal.

"I whispered in their ears, urging them to commit a murder to which they were already inclined, killing them at their most vulnerable moment. I extend the same warning to you as I did

55

to your parents… either you serve me and release me from this grave, or I will rise up and destroy everything you hold dear. Your life is shining bright and your road is fully paved, but that can end in a moment. Jatara, just remember how many master sorcerers and millennia it took to confine me… do you really think that you can stop me? I only need to acquire one kosher soul to return to the surface, you, your unconceived child, or some other descendant of yours… I am patient. I will obtain what I need. It is inevitable. I am Derideon… a god below ground. The Creator made me, but couldn't control me. Do you truly think that an insignificant sorcerer's daughter will be able to resist me?"

Jatara and her army were pressing forward through the woods as Derideon's voice boomed around them. The tree-dwellers joined them, descending from the trees with in celebration, although the voice of Derideon caused them to cower behind the elite soldiers who remained.

Jatara responded to his tyrannical inquisition once more, not wanting to show weakness before her troops. "Derideon, you are the Creator's greatest mistake, and I have been sent to vanquish you.

"Unlike the Creator, I don't have any compassion, love or pity for you. Destroying you will be a pleasure. You are a deceiver and a mutilator of mankind. I have only been alive for two decades and have contributed to your ruin more than anyone before me. The Creator gave us all powers, but yours were used to devastate and exterminate innocent people for your own sadistic, depraved pleasure. Derideon, you're no more than a parasite feeding on the souls of men, and giving them nothing in return. Your time will come, and your death will be at my hand."

Jatara, her troops, and one hundred tree-dwellers exited the forest. The remaining tree-dwellers stayed behind to rebuild their kingdom, which was now under her command. After their departure, they heard a bombastic bellowing from beneath the earth, as Derideon once again swore to enact revenge upon Jatara. Then, silence reigned from below.

The tree-dwellers joined her army, leaving her with thirty-five hundred soldiers at her command. The next kingdom surrendered immediately upon her approach, lining the streets with gifts and food, and even organizing festivities in her honor. Jatara was invited into the king's sanctuary, where his son and wife also resided.

Jatara and her army were pleased to receive treatment befitting royalty; they were bathed, massaged and fed the finest foods, provided the most lavish drinks, and shown to exceptional accommodations. After they were fed and pampered, Jatara met with the king, in the company of her entourage.

She took fifty of her elite warriors, lightly armed, as she didn't see these people as a threat. King Valdon, Queen Meshonda and their son, Prince Kardale, sat in a row of thrones, with an empty throne between them, reserved for Jatara.

King Valdon initiated the conversation. "Jatara, on behalf of my family and kingdom, we welcome you into our domain. We don't wish to fight, but to unite. Please join us. You can become my son's wife and this kingdom's princess. It would be an enormous honor to all of us."

Queen Meshonda desperately hoped for Jatara's acceptance into her family's empire, and offered her own lofty words. "Jatara, we have known about you for years and have made numerous attempts to reach you. Unfortunately, we failed, due to the forest that lies at the edge of our kingdom, where thousands of our brave soldiers lost their lives in attempts to contact you. When our watchmen reported that you had survived the obstacles in that deadly place, we were elated, relieved and impressed that you were able to endure and emerge victorious over Derideon's forces. We are endlessly honored that you would grace us with your presence, but you no longer have to face these obstacles alone. Please, accept my offer to become my daughter-in-law. Jatara, we will worship you forever. We will gladly submit our souls to you... this very day."

Prince Kardale was the next to articulate his desires and argue for her hand in marriage. "I am a man of strapping proportions, able to satisfy your demands both on the battlefield and in the bedroom. I'm twenty-three years old, but have earned my place as a captain, master swordsman and elite archer for our army. I have fought and led more battles against the ground-dwellers and Demon knights than the years in my life. I did all of that with the sole intent of overcoming those obstacles to behold and speak to you. I truly admire your military prowess; you are an excellent captain, sorceress and warrior. Jatara, I have longed for the moment when I could stand before you and witness your beauty. That moment is finally here. Allow me the honor of fathering your lineage. I would be greatly honored if you merely consider my request, your majesty."

Jatara was overwhelmed by the offers being made by the same people who had so easily surrendered their power, souls and kingdom into her possession. She needed time to consider what motives they had, if any, aside from the preservation of their lives and those of their citizens.

After some thought, Jatara replied coldly. "None of you are in the position to offer me anything. You surrendered before I had the chance to conquer you. However, the hospitality you and your kingdom have bestowed on my soldiers and I is admirable. Therefore, I have entertained your request. From this day forward, I will be your ruler, and my name is to be praised by every soul in this kingdom. Prince Kardale is indeed a viable and handsome mate. After careful review of his prominence and stature, I may let him father my child, who would be his ruler, never to be viewed as an equal. That status is earned, not offered. I appreciate the kindness that has been shown to me, but don't mistake my gratitude for stupidity. I am to be worshipped, not patronized. Three expansive kingdoms are now under my possession, giving praise to my name at this very moment. This kingdom will be the fourth that I control, so step down from those thrones, bow down before me and worship my name. Then, I may spare your lives, along with the lives of your people."

The king, queen, and prince, although taken aback, immediately obeyed her commands, swearing that their subjects would do the same. Jatara liked the obeisance of these conquered subjects, and decided to use this kingdom as her base of operations as she expanded across the eastern hemisphere.

*

A little over three years later, Jatara left the shores of Australia, sailing back to Europe in her fleet of tactical war ships. After a number of exhausting campaigns, she decided to rest for a bit upon her return.

As she stepped back onto Europe's banks, Prince Kardale was there to greet her with a stunning white stallion, while he sat astride a black one.

After years of dutiful servitude, Jatara was ready for him to father her child; she was twenty-four and Kardale was twenty-seven; the time was right to create an heir. She confidently held fifty kingdoms under her rule, but the exorbitant number of sieges had been accomplished in a shockingly short span of time.

However, to keep Derideon's influence at a minimum, the western hemisphere still need to be secured, which was an endeavor she would pursue after birthing an heir to her vast empire.

Everything seemed to be in order; a new palace was being built for Jatara and Kardale, who she had deemed worthy, and was genuinely eager for him to play an active role in her child's life. Within two months of moving into their new palace, Jatara was with child, a revelation that elated her tremendously.

She positively glowed at the prospect of being a mother, as she deeply yearned for a soul to nurture and love. Just as her parents had doted on her constantly, she could now reciprocate those blessings on her baby. Weeks passed and Jatara took on a more motherly role, just as Shabella had, leaving her generals and chief lieutenants in charge of protecting and managing the nations under her influence and command.

By the time she reached her sixth month of pregnancy, her unborn child had enough clothes and blankets so that none of them would ever be worn more than once. The finest garments filled the baby's room – silk and gold linen, diamonds for buttons… no expense was spared.

The crib was solid gold, studded with rubies and diamonds, causing the room to shine like stars in the sky. Kardale wanted to name the baby; if it was a boy, he wanted to name it after his Uncle Kardon, a mighty warrior who had fought in the great battle against Derideon's soldiers when they tried to take over King Valdon's previous kingdom.

Kardon had led the army that drove Derideon's demonic forces back into the forest, but he and his troops had been overcome by Demon knights and the death pits, where they had been impaled, burned and eaten alive by the hellhounds. Their valiant, suicidal efforts had kept Derideon's army from advancing further, and he was unable to gain strength from their deaths by retrieving their souls, like the many tree-dwellers who had chosen to give over their souls.

Kardon and his soldiers had fought for the protection and survival of their nation, making it a fight for justice, and refused to surrender their souls to him. Instead, they accepted their death in battle, which made it impossible for Derideon to extract their essence.

Jatara respected the memory of Kardon's valor and self-sacrifice, which she had heard about not only from Kardale and his parents, but also from the citizens, who had erected marble, brass and gold statues of the legendary man throughout the kingdom.

Given all that, Jatara had no problem considering *Kardon* as the potential name of her child. Aside from that, Jatara had many other choices to make regarding her future ambitions. She often wondered whether it was sensible to move on to the western hemisphere and decrease the power of Derideon's supporters.

It needed to be done, but she wondered whether she could relinquish such a large contingent of soldiers to pursue such an arduous task without her help, as she was approaching her due date. As her pregnancy advanced, she became less mobile, and was more of a liability to her soldiers on the battlefield.

Jatara could feel an imminent threat approaching, even before word reached her about a horde of invading tribes and armies from the Western hemisphere, proclaiming their allegiance to Derideon. They were pushing closer to the Eastern hemisphere, threatening the lands and kingdoms she had secured; a fierce battle was inevitable.

Her greatest concern wasn't the impending war that would take place; it was only a matter of time. However, she doubted that she would have enough strength to protect her troops from the massive army. The pregnancy had weakened Jatara's powers significantly, leaving her nation vulnerable to such a large attacking force of demons.

There was no way for her to protect all her kingdoms in her present condition. Her army of sixty thousand was multiplied to a force of eighty thousand when Jatara enhanced the strength of her elite forces, giving those warriors powers that no other mortal possessed, but she would be unable to stand on the frontlines with them.

In the months that followed, Derideon's army increased to ninety thousand Demon Knights. These fiends were half-demon and hell-bent on killing, wreaking carnage as they swept across the countryside like a plague, demolishing crops and livestock, extinguishing the population, and leaving a wake of pestilence in their path. Jatara's weakened abilities ensured safe passage for the invasion force, and her soldiers were being mangled in the field.

It was a futile war for Jatara's army, pitching man against beast, and her men were being mercilessly slaughtered by Derideon's destructive slaves. The legion of killers was drawing near to Jatara's last stronghold in the East. She was protected by her remaining reserve of elite soldiers, empowered by her sorcery. They were also highly trained in extreme combat, but she feared it wouldn't be enough.

She poured all the energy she could spare into her troops, but it was greatly reduced, as she had to maintain her life force to sustain her pregnancy and survive the labor to come.

Derideon kept his promise to Jatara; he had assembled a massive army of Demon Knights to conquer her and take the lands she ruled. For a moment, Derideon's demonic purpose had crossed her mind – the possession of her unborn child.

However, Jatara was defiant, having achieved too much to give up so easily. She set up a fortified barrier to ward off the advance of Derideon's forces. Even though he was not there physically, his presence was felt through the immense approaching army. The Demon Knights had penetrated the city's outer retaining wall, where they met Jatara's elite force of ten thousand. Prince Kardale fought bravely, holding back the opposing army and giving Jatara a chance to flee.

Unfortunately, her condition was progressing and the labor pains had begun. The baby was on its way and Jatara had no option to escape. Derideon's army was kept contained for as long as possible; but they eventually penetrated Jatara's defenses. A small band of survivors retreated to alert Jatara of their brutal defeat…

CHAPTER 7

The retreating soldiers were bloodied and exhausted when they reached her. They addressed Jatara within the fortress, which was guarded by a dozen of her most elite sentinels.

"My lady, we couldn't contain these savage hellions. They are advancing towards you as we speak. One of the creatures is possessed by Derideon's spirit. It commands his forces, sending his killers to destroy our remaining soldiers. We battled valiantly, slaying thousands of Demon Knights, but we were overwhelmed by their immensity. Only eighty of us survived. We stand before you now to offer our lives in your defense."

Jatara was honored by her army's courageous effort, even though they had failed. She knew that their defeat was due to her impending birth, as she had been able to give them only limited assistance.

Jatara was about to deliver at any moment. She was so proud of her warriors, but was enraged that she couldn't protect or assist them in battle. These men had fought with her since the beginning of her conquest. Jatara didn't want anyone else to suffer her plight, so she released them from their duty. Only the midwives remained to help in the delivery.

Jatara spoke to her soldiers somberly. "I am proud of you all for serving me with such dignity, valor and strength. I want everyone here to make it back to their families alive, to enjoy the rest of your lives with the ones you love. My baby is nearly here, as is my nemesis. Leave while you still can. Take the remaining citizens that haven't already evacuated and leave. I command you."

As Jatara finished, with a final mighty push, the baby arrived – a baby boy that was placed in his mother's embrace. The men gave their blessing and exited the room, leaving Jatara alone, as requested.

As she was preparing to nurse her baby for the first time, she heard the sound of Derideon's troops approaching. She hadn't the power or strength to defend herself, and in her desperation, she pulled out a dagger to take her newborn child's life, but could not do it after looking at the magnificent infant.

His father had been slain in the battle to protect the fortress, meaning that it was up to her to decide her son's fate and confront Derideon.

Regardless of her impending doom, she was not afraid to challenge her adversary for a final time. Without warning, it happened. The iron doors that sealed her sanctuary were rammed with such intensity that they bent off their hinges and collapsed to the floor. The room was immediately filled with Demon Knights, blocking any final chance of escape.

A smoking abomination entered the room, claiming to be Derideon's avatar, saying that it spoke and acted on his master's commands. He boasted to the exhausted woman on the bed; after Derideon's demon legion had possessed ten million souls, his master could once more walk the earth.

The avatar spoke in a deep, demonic voice, "I gave you many chances to surrender and praise me, but now you leave me no choice. I came to take your son and the remainder of your life force. You would have served as my chief lieutenant, standing at my right hand, but now you will perish. Your child will take that title instead. Now, give me what is mine or I will snatch his head from that tiny body, and you will witness his birth and death in the same hour."

Jatara took his threat seriously, and chose not to antagonize Derideon any further. She did not want to jeopardize her child's life. She had no idea what the baby's future would hold, as events had truly spiraled into an unexpected abyss. *Would her son become a mindless drone, acting under Derideon's control, or would he be defiant and rise up against this oppressive dictator?*

Either way would be a better fate than her son being slaughtered before he had a chance to walk. Jatara relinquished her son, whom she had named Kragon, after her grandfather, one of the legendary sorcerers responsible for ousting Derideon, ultimately condemning him to the underworld.

This fact eluded Derideon, who was unaware that Kragon his associate was instrumental in his imprisonment, so when Jatara called her son Kragon, the name was accepted by Derideon parasitic being, who was a host to carry out his malicious plots of destruction.

The fiendish specter talked in a crude, distorted voice of hisses and grunts. "Your time will end here today, Jatara. Your son will become my son. Demons, destroy her! Leave nothing to be discovered. Burn this palace to the ground and bring her ashes to me."

With that, Derideon's minion exited the expansive room with the baby in hand, wrapped in a fleece blanket trimmed with gold and silk, disappearing into the hall where he descended the tower steps.

A loud explosion rocked the building as he exited, followed by fire and smoke. Brick and mortar cascaded out from the palace, but one Demon Knight spoke to the avatar, as he had been thrown from an upper window.

"What transpired... is unclear..." he mumbled to his master. "The woman spoke... in a foreign language... one I knew not... her body... glowed. She sent a burst of energy... it incinerated the room... I saw... only flames and smoke... nothing could have survived." The Demon Knight was nearly gone, but the avatar picked him up with a clenched fist and shouted into his face."

"I entrusted a deed to your hands, but there is no proof here that Jatara is dead. For your sake, pray she has expired. If not, I will tear you to shreds, slowly… for decades."

Looking up at the smoking rubble of the tower, which had collapsed in on itself, Derideon's minion was confident that the great mission had been successful.

*

As such, he turned his attention to Kragon, who needed nourishment. He clumsily placed the infant in a basket to carry and strode into the conquered city.

He sought out a wet nurse and came across a woman named Latonga working the streets of the city, petitioning for any available work. The provinces were largely vacant now, with only a few stragglers left within the kingdom. This buxom woman had once worked as a wet nurse for the royal families of the region. Derideon's avatar told her who Kragon was, and who he represented, and she agreed to serve him.

As they made their way to the underworld, Derideon's host body began to deteriorate. It no longer could handle the demands placed upon it, so it handed Kragon to Latonga, then instructed her to proceed into the nearby cave, where she and the baby would enter a portal that led into the realms of the underworld. The minion began to convulse violently, and dark fluid poured from its ears and mouth.

Then, the demon's voice stopped. Nothing but an eerie silence filled the air as the corpse dropped at the mouth of the cavern. Latonga nursed Kragon as she entered the damp, pungent void, and stepped through a vortex near the back of the tunnel.

As she and the baby exited the swirling funnel, they were met by an imposing figure standing beside an immense column of stone. As this enormous man approached, he said that his name was Derideon, the same one that had given her and the baby the privilege to serve him. In addition, he promised that as long as she remained a loyal servant, she would have a lofty position in his kingdom to come.

Derideon confidently explained the conditions of Latonga's obligations to Kragon, and what he demanded of her. "I am now the alpha and omega in your life. You will abide by my rule. You will also nurture and feed Kragon until he is six years old. Thereafter, I will mold him into the instrument of devastation he will be, delivering incredible feats of destruction on those who resist my ascent. I will teach him the art of deception, and how to cleverly manipulate and control mankind, for he must win the hearts of man if I am to possess enough souls to return to the surface and escape this earthly prison.

"Kragon will be my greatest student. He will be trained by me for thousands of years, or at least until people have forgotten about me. I cannot exit through the vortex you entered, but you and Kragon can pass back into the world above. I am confined here until I have acquired the souls I need, ten million, which will take Kragon hundreds of years to accomplish. When the time is right, he will be released upon the world to accomplish his mission. If Jatara had joined my regime, I could free myself of this imprisonment much sooner. No matter, now I must be patient and shape my son, Kragon, in my likeness, teaching him everything I know about sorcery, including the forbidden language of *kabar*, the speech that locked me here. Perhaps he will someday be able to reverse the spell that his family, that evil sect of sorcerers, once placed on me.

"Your majesty, I only wish to serve you. I know of your might, and I am honored to be your servant. Kragon is of majestic blood, which means that he can live for thousands of years, particularly given his mother, the indomitable Jatara, and her parents, the Almighty Econ and Shabella. To serve you as you ask, I would also need to extend my life, just like them. Can you provide me that, Lord Derideon?

"Latonga, I can't promise you an extended life after you have served me for six years, but I will grant you power and prestige in my kingdom if you serve me well. When I found you on the corner, you were nothing more than a lactating whore, working the streets for food and money. You are in no position to request anything. You are lucky to be alive and have the chance to serve me. I have given your life purpose; without my

67

intervention, disease and starvation would have been your only reward. I will give no recompense, Latonga, without your services being rendered in full to my kingdom, which you have sworn to serve."

"I am a loyal servant, Derideon, and will serve you obediently. I do not mean to seem ungrateful. Serving you is the greatest honor. I will care for Kragon like my own son, who is ten years old and lives with his father. They both fled the city after your army conquered Jatara's kingdom. I stayed to collect any valuables left behind, and look for any lucrative opportunities that may arise under a new ruler. Before the city fell, I nursed rich patrons' children, and slept with their husbands, knowingly or unknowingly, for the right price. I thank you, Derideon, for this opportunity. I will never forget it and will remain grateful. I hope that my name may be remembered as the provider of life for your most valuable warrior, Kragon."

Latonga had gladly accepted her role as the caretaker of the baby, and Derideon trusted her experience, dedication and credentials. He allowed her to travel back and forth freely through the portal with supplies and food so that she could care for and nurse the baby.

When Kragon was one year old, he was allowed to go above ground with Latonga to experience sunlight and fresh circulating air, which was needed for him to develop properly into a healthy man. Latonga suggested this to Derideon and he reluctantly agreed with her. He worried that the child would get confused and sick due to the extreme environmental changes, but Latonga presented a firm argument. The world to which he was confined was much different from what the surface provided. His surroundings offered minimum sunlight, only the small amount that refracted through the vortex leading from the portal. There were only minute air pockets seeping below ground, providing just enough oxygen for the occupants who dwelled in that underground prison.

Derideon had forgotten how uninviting his home really was; he had resided there for several millennia, eating whatever his worshippers brought him. Anyone who stumbled into his home became a servant of his regime. His dwelling was roughly the size of a Roman pantheon, with large pillars holding up the crumbling ceiling, which consisted of massive stone slabs stretching overhead. It was essentially a soul eradication field, where his Demon Knights could train and prepare for battle. Tens of thousands of creatures had died on that ground – man and demon alike. The stench inside the cave was agonizing, an aroma of old, decomposing flesh and ancient blood.

It was a breeding ground for death and desolation. After fighters were killed, they were thrown back through the vortex, which ejected them inside the cave. The men who fought and died for Derideon were his worshippers, so he used sinister spells to mutate them into half-man hybrid beasts. These unfortunate souls were mixed with bears, wolves and lions – horrific abominations doomed to walk the earth. They were bold and ferocious, slaughtering anything that crossed their path. These beasts were nearly indestructible; only Econ had been able to stop them in the battle waged between he and Derideon eons earlier.

As the years passed, Latonga and Kragon were allowed to venture further outside the cave, although they were not permitted to journey far without Kasmal, the powerful demon Knight who had been taught and mentored by Derideon. Kasmal was Derideon's most trusted guard and executioner. Kragon was now three years old, growing into a playful, energetic and rambunctious child.

Latonga was now feeding him solid food and weaning him off breast milk. He was a very inquisitive child, asking questions about everything he saw. The more he matured, the more his mind became aware of his surroundings. He could spot a deer hiding behind a tree thirty yards out.

Kragon was also overdeveloped for his age; at three, he looked like a six-year-old, with the speed and agility to match. Despite his physical advancement, Derideon was concerned with his social development; he didn't want him to socialize with people who he would need to learn how to conquer and control. Although he was still just a child, it was important for Derideon to establish a barrier for Kragon between he and others.

Kragon's interaction with other children was extremely limited. Derideon wanted his prized student to feel superior to all others, allowing him to separate himself from his peers, which wasn't difficult to accomplish, considering his size, strength and aptitude. To Derideon's dismay, a lot of Jatara and Prince Kardale could be seen in Kragon's appearance.

Derideon was incredibly methodical about what Kragon learned; he knew that he would grow up to be a vastly powerful adult, so Derideon needed to mold him while he was still impressionable. If he waited until he was older, it would be too late to influence the incalculable force that Kragon would become.

Three more years passed in much the same way, and Kragon was now six years old. Latonga had served faithfully and was ready to collect on her services rendered. "Derideon, I have carried out your will. I nurtured and fed the child for six years; he sees me as his mother, and at times, I feel that I am. Kragon is growing up fast, and has many questions that I cannot answer. He asks why you are trapped in a cave, and, if you are his father, why don't you practice falconry with him in the fields, like the other fathers play with their sons. I usually tell him that you're busy with your studies, and then Kasmal and I take him out to play. Your majesty, what do you ask of me, since my tenure serving as Kragon's wet nurse is finished? You once promised me power and prestige, although the honor of serving you has been enough. Do with me as you see fit, for I am your humble servant who is eager to obey your request."

"Rise to your feet, Latonga. The conviction you've shown is impressive, and you have been a valuable addition to my endeavors. I know that you will continue to serve me well. As a sign of my gratitude, and expectation of future service, I will extend your life by two hundred years. The rejuvenation spell will be performed at dusk on the night that Kragon reaches the age of fourteen. I need him to assist me with a particular piece of twisted sorcery, and he must offer me a small portion of his blood. However, he is not yet mature enough to participate in the ritual, which would require him to speak in *kabar*. That innate ability only comes with maturity. Speak freely, Latonga…

what do you wish to do? When he comes of age, your life will be extended for your service to me and the child. You do not need to stay here. I will honor that agreement."

"I want to remain here, my lord, for I have grown fond of the boy. I also like the protection that you and Kasmal provide. I have nowhere to go, and only hope that you will allow me to stay. I could continue acting as a motherly figure for Kragon. After you discovered me, I was given a means to exist with purpose, rather than just surviving. I have been able to help, even in a small way, in your quest to return to the surface and reclaim your seat as ruler. I only wish to serve you, Derideon."

"Your request is admirable, but I will not allow you to interfere or influence Kragon any further. He must be a merciless killer, capable of the most malicious forms of manipulation. Latonga, if you shower him with too much affection, I will be unable to harden him into the heartless dictator that I need to lead my crusade. Kragon must be unsympathetic, ruthless, and obedient to only one master. He doesn't need two minds to rule his. You may stay as a surrogate mother, but every choice you make concerning him must be approved by me. I need him to lead my army, so that we can both taste victory. Latonga, you have served me well, and will continue to do so if you remain. I am the emperor of this domain; my approval of your deeds should be paramount in your life. Earning your lord's satisfaction is key to your survival. If you want to survive, you will allow me to shape this child as I see fit, and stay out of my way."

Latonga shivered, but nodded obediently.

CHAPTER 8

In the year 1120, Kragon turned fourteen. It was finally time to begin teaching him the ways of a demon knight. However, Derideon wanted him to be much more than a soldier; he wanted Kragon to be a masterful sorcerer. In order for this to occur, he would have to gain Kragon's trust and loyalty.

Derideon sought to do this by befriending the boy, showing an interest in his activities and making him feel as comfortable as possible, in an attempt to create a conducive learning environment.

A few months after Kragon turned fourteen, Derideon summoned the boy, so Latonga brought the young man to his chambers. Kragon was intensely curious about all matters of life and their workings and asked dozens of questions every day. At the feet of his surrogate father, his curiosity did not waver. "Derideon, are you my father? Or are you my master, with control over my life and destiny? People on the surface say that you are not my father, but if that's true, then who are you?"

Taken aback by the boy's forward questioning, Derideon did not answer immediately. "I am... Derideon, your father and master. You are a child who will grow up to make his father proud. Kragon, your parents were killed in a battle protecting their kingdom. I was also there, but not in this physical form. I acquired the body of one of my followers, but only a few of us survived – you and me. At that point, you were just a suckling infant, which is why I asked Latonga to care for you and provide the love and care a young child needs. Kragon, I took you in as my own son, but now it's time for you to fulfill your destiny... as the most powerful warrior and sorcerer in my army."

"Father, is my destiny only what you have decided it to be, or can I choose my own?"

"I saved your life, Kragon. To repay me for ensuring your survival, I need you to release me from this tomb to which I have been condemned. Understand this, son... anything done in life for another is performed for ulterior motives. The woman you call your mother performs her duty for personal gain, but you will repay Latonga today... her long wait has ended. I have a rejuvenation spell that I need your help to cast. Latonga gave you those scrolls to awaken your natural abilities to master *kabar*. Now that you have started on this path, the ceremony will be done solely by you. Although I can speak the language of this magic, it's limited to enhancing soulless beings and rotting corpses – a crippling curse attached to my entrapment. However, you can decipher and speak in *kabar*, even at a young age, which is typically an ability reserved for seasoned master sorcerers. Kragon, you will reward Latonga for nourishing you and finalize the debt you owe for your existence; all you need to do is offer a small portion of your life fluid during the recitation of the spell. I rescued you from certain death, due to your stupendous potential, but all the power in the world means nothing unless you can learn to control it."

Kragon was overflowing with more questions about Derideon, mainly how he was acquainted with his parents, and whether were they close. "Derideon, I could call you father, but you are not. You have admitted that, and have told me that the only reason you didn't let me perish was my intrinsic value as a royal servant to your ascent. I wish to know more about my parents... were they like me? Are they responsible for my abilities? How did you come to know of them? Do you know the story of their lives?"

"Kragon, you remind me a great deal of your mother, who was highly inquisitive at a very young age. Furthermore, she was a powerful sorceress that conquered many kingdoms and numerous nations. I knew your parents well, especially Jatara, whose reputation was known around the world. Your father was Prince Kardale, the son of king Valdon, whose kingdom was dominated by Jatara and her soldiers. My relationship with your mother was minimal. I served in her elite army brigade as a military advisor; she consulted with me telepathically for my expertise, which is how I was able to rescue you when Jatara and Kardale were overthrown by an army of nefarious sorcerers. She sent word to me, so I possessed a host demon knight to find you and then fled with you to safety. I have heard many stories about your mother's abilities as a child. It was said that she could speak *kabar* by the age of six, and could converse with any scholar on a vast range of topics... she was wise far beyond her years. You are of the same stock, Kragon."

Derideon waited for another barrage of questions, but it didn't come, and he felt a wave of relief. "Now that you know that you know a bit about your past, it's time to begin moving on the path to your future. I will train you in the tactics of warfare and sorcery, enabling you to rule over the inhabitants of the earth. First, you must rule over the terrain. People must eat to survive, so if you control their food intake and land on which to produce it, the battle is already won..."

"Derideon, why can't you free yourself from this underground lair? How is it possible that I have the dominion to release you?" Kragon asked boldly, clearly not finished with his queries.

"I can't escape this subterranean chamber on my own. I need someone of great power to retrieve and collect the souls from the surface to break this containment spell that has been placed upon me by my enemies. They are the same sorcerers responsible for your parents' death, and the destruction of their kingdom. It took over two hundred master sorcerers to bind me, but nothing is permanent. Kragon, with your assistance, I will be liberated and our adversaries will be torn asunder. "

Latonga and Kasmal were exiting the vortex just as Derideon was finishing his speech to Kragon. Turning his attention towards them, he asked of their whereabouts, and whether they had returned with enough food rations to last the week.

Kasmal reassured Derideon that their mission had been a success, confirmed by the four massive sacks he had dragged through the portal, which contained one deer, two boars, and forty apples. Latonga added a keg of fresh cow milk for Kragon to the inventory.

All of these perishable items, including the game animals, were placed near the back of the pantheon wall, which was very cold, due to the depth of the structure. It never exceeded fifty degrees, so food could stay fresh until it was consumed.

Derideon was satisfied with their performance and motioned both of them to come towards him. "You have both done well. Kasmal, you can eat your fill of bloody meat after you have skinned and butchered the game, which Latonga will then prepare. After finishing your meal, go into the villages and satisfy yourself with the harlots. It is dusk now, but return before midnight. Latonga, your rejuvenation spell will be performed tonight. I told you that you would be compensated for your labor, and that promise will be honored," Derideon finished.

Kasmal finished his meal, sharpened his sword and promptly exited through the vortex. Derideon was ready to begin the ritual. He instructed Latonga to bring his platinum dagger with the gold handle. Kragon stood beside him and was given a scroll to read; at the completion of his articulation of the text in *kabar*, the spell required him to cut his left hand and let a drop of blood fall into her mouth, which would finalize the spell.

Latonga began convulsing as the blood entered her mouth and she fell into a deep sleep. The spell was taking effect and Kragon had officially begun his journey to higher development. He had successfully used *kabar*, a language that only a master sorcerer should have been able to perform, a person of much greater experience and age than himself.

Derideon was very impressed by Kragon's abilities. He knew that this young man would grow up to be an overwhelming warrior and the sorcerer who could help him regain his freedom.

Kragon was also feeling very energized after performing the rejuvenation ritual. He could sense the power he possessed, but wanted to feel even more, so he asked Derideon to give him some additional spells to study, recite and learn. Kragon was eager to increase his knowledge, which was precisely the response that Derideon wanted from Kragon – an insatiable hunger for power and domination.

Nonetheless, he knew that the boy needed to rest after such an ordeal, so he instead directed him to his sleeping chambers, promising to provide the boy with more spells soon. Kragon was off to sleep within minutes. On the contrary, Latonga began to awake from her unconsciousness, feeling revitalized and jubilant. Two hundred years had been added to her life and she felt invincible, full of vigor and energy, as if her life would never end.

After rising to her feet, she walked toward Derideon to show homage and respect for her savior, for the man who had extended her life. She began to speak to him in a humble and grateful manner. "I deeply appreciate what you have done for me, Derideon. I feel nearly immortal, thanks to you, my Lord. As I stand before you, refreshed and renewed, I dedicate the rest of my existence and service to you."

"I will call upon you when your help is needed, Latonga. Until then, go out onto the world with Kasmal and spread my good name. Tell them how merciful and generous I am, and how they will be rewarded for worshipping my name. In the meantime, you must repair the damage that Jatara did by refusing to praise me. She was defiant to the end, which made her a martyr of rebellion. I know that she will still have followers, those who worship her even as a god. These factions must be rooted out and exterminated, as they compromise our mission to spread my gospel and agenda. Kasmal, you have returned at the beginning of your command detail, which entails vanquishing anyone who doesn't accept my doctrine."

Derideon had accomplished his first objective, as far as earning the respect and trust of his immediate subjects, who were willing to do whatever it took to please him and help with his conquest of the world.

76

That night, Kragon dreamt of power; imagining his use of *kabar* to articulate advanced spells enthralled him. Learning from Derideon became Kragon's passion and imitating his father figure was an obsession that steadily progressed with every passing month.

Latonga and Kasmal had many questions for Derideon concerning how they should proceed with influencing the masses that had previously been converted to Jatara's regime and were loyal followers of her dynasty. He responded with brute force and intimidation, as he had so many times in the past. Derideon also stated that this was the only way people had bent to his control in the past, which was why Kragon was so essential to his undertaking. Through him, diplomatic persuasion and force would be introduced to persuade the population to worship and follow him, enabling their souls to be procured without violence.

Derideon realized that it was more effective to win the people's hearts through persuasion, rather than the use of unadulterated force, which would result in more hostility and greater resistance. Derideon instructed Kasmal to use less force, and told Latonga that the enhancement spell not only extended her life, but also provided a small amount of power to execute certain spells upon his command. He also instructed them to display their powers and abilities in public, so that others would desire their gifts. He ordered that his followers tell all those who inquired about his power that Derideon had provided that power, and that if the masses worshipped him, the same would be offered to them.

Latonga and Kasmal had been given their orders, along with their other duties of maintaining the home front. They went out on daily missions to locate and minister to the surrounding villages near the cave. Their excursions were never greater than a dozen miles, since they were limited in terms of numbers and resources to carry out an extended campaign. In due time, as their followers increased, they would be able to spread Derideon's doctrine across many nations, capturing souls by the tens of thousands, helping their lord reach the ultimate goal of world domination.

He knew that he had to gain his freedom to pursue his ultimate ambitions. Latonga was the brain and orator of the operation, while Kasmal represented a physical presence as a bona fide enforcer. Together, they converted hundreds of people to the worship of Derideon, who relinquished their essence to him, either by force or persuasion. Many of these unfortunate souls simply needed someone to believe in.

Faith in Jatara was no longer an option, so it was easy to coerce them to follow a new, more radical and parasitic allegiance, that took life from its members without actually enhancing their existence. Derideon used the same principles as Jatara had, namely siphoning energy from the souls of others to increase his life force and spell-casting power.

In contrast, her followers had been conscious and coherent, unlike the transformation into depraved, blood-thirsty monstrosities that Derideon's converts faced. Kasmal was no exception to this fate. All of Derideon's followers were doomed to this condemnation after submitting their souls. Even Latonga was forced to change in appearance, but only slightly, as Derideon needed her to appeal to the public by looking less threatening.

On the other hand, Kasmal was a Chief Demon knight, bearing fangs, rippling muscles and sharp claws, standing over six feet tall and armed with two razor-edge serrated swords. He wore a battle-axe on his hip and was dressed in a loincloth beneath an iron breastplate and shield attached to his forearm. Derideon's worshippers were entranced in a debilitating state, unable to act or think on their own without his command.

However, Derideon wouldn't inflict this condition on Kragon; his soul was too valuable a commodity to be extracted, considering that his job was to collect souls with his strategic sorcery. That task would eventually release Derideon from bondage, but could certainly not be accomplished if Kragon was a mindless drone.

Derideon gave Kragon full access to his collection of spells and conjurations, and there were only a few he couldn't decipher. As time passed, Kragon became more and more astute at sorcery; he was able to conjure and read complex spells by the age of seventeen. Three years after enacting his first rejuvenation spell to enhance Latonga's life, Kragon was becoming restless. He wanted more responsibility and a higher rank in this swelling militia, formed with the sole purpose of releasing their benefactor to rule once more.

The young man was eager to play an important role in the new kingdom, and Derideon had promised that he would be a key factor in the expansion of his empire. Derideon's extreme sect was gaining ground in the surrounding villages and those villagers were spreading his doctrine to more distant kingdoms. Many swore to never commit, but the tide was spreading throughout the area. Those who did worship Derideon were often ousted from their kingdoms for worshipping gods not recognized by their cultures.

This expulsion of Derideon's followers unexpectedly resulted in them being dispersed to other nations, allowing them to spread their messages and beliefs to unfamiliar inhabitants. Derideon needed this caustic ministry of worship to travel throughout the Americas. However, he would have to wait until technology and Kragon had advanced enough for that to occur.

In the meantime, Derideon sought to establish his teachings in Africa, beginning in Egypt, and then continue his perverse campaign in Europe, converting as many souls as possible. Latonga's new lease on life was solely dedicated to exalting and advocating her benefactor everywhere she went. Kasmal also remained valuable to Derideon, as that virulent behemoth was a one-demon army who protected Latonga on her journeys to convert the populace.

Villagers began to submit in ever-larger numbers, due to Latonga's command of illusions and spells, which tricked the untrained eyes of onlookers, along with Kasmal's undeniable strength and ferocity, which Derideon had bestowed upon him. This was not the only sorcery he infused within his two leading disciples; their unwavering support was the result of an obedience spell he had cast, unbeknownst to them.

Derideon needed Latonga and Kasmal's unyielding loyalty to his cause without draining his life force, which was instead needed to control his growing army of drones. In the past, when he had a legion of Demon Knights, their souls could be taken and converted into energy, leaving nothing but a shell of pestilence to carry out his savagery. Therefore, he had an ample supply of energy while overthrowing Jatara, but his army and reserve of power had been depleted by her elite forces. Despite that, she eventually succumbed to her weakened state and the sheer volume of Demon Knights.

Derideon spent hours each day with Kragon, teaching him the rules of war and instructing him on how to conjure powerful spells. Derideon had no knowledge of how to decipher or pronounce the intricate pieces of sorcery. He had acquired them by looting Kragon's family millennia ago, waiting for his bloodline to open their secrets… those same descendants who had once banded together, calling themselves the "Vindicators", and banished him in the earth.

Although he could read some text in *kabar*, other scripts of greater significance were indiscernible to him; this was all the result of his curse and exile into the bowels of the world. However, Kragon could articulate and execute these more sophisticated scrolls with flawless accuracy, developing him as an unconquerable force that only became stronger with time.

His ability was innate. Kragon's majestic wizarding background made him impossible to control, so Derideon's only hope of utilizing this austere young titan was by deceit and manipulation, his personal specialty.

Years cascaded by and Kragon reach the age of twenty-two, equipped with the physical development of a herculean man and the intellectual attributes of a master sorcerer. He was a sage capable of masterfully commanding troops of any number or ability. He was a natural leader and a willing soldier for Derideon – a decision that would later haunt him.

CHAPTER 9

Derideon was enamored by Kragon's abilities, although it was increasingly difficult to quell his energy and ambitions each day. It was becoming a true challenge for Derideon to find things that could captivate and occupy Kragon's mind.

Eventually, the young savant became restless and introspective, and then began asking a stream of questions relating to his status in Derideon's evolving empire. "Why am I given less obligations and more restrictions than Latonga and Kasmal? I have abilities that they can't even comprehend, yet I remain locked away, unable to use these talents and powers on any quest of theirs. Derideon, I mean no disrespect, but even you can't perform these advanced spell incantations... something that has come to me without much effort or tutelage. I ask myself many questions to which I can find no answers. I can only assume that they lie with you, if you feel gracious enough to provide me with the truth. You have taught me to be a dominator of men, I know hundreds of ways to weaken and conquer a nation, but to what end? Is it only to benefit you and your quest for world domination? Where do I fit? And how am I to profit from this conquest?"

Derideon was highly agitated by Kragon's outburst. However, he knew better than to express his anger, knowing that it would cause division, rather than unity, between them. That was something Derideon wanted to avoid at all costs. He was very cautious when answering Kragon, "I understand your frustration, Kragon. You are searching for answers to questions that perplex you. It's true that you do have certain endowments that Latonga and Kasmal lack, and they will never be able to accomplish the momentous feats that you will someday achieve. However, I know this isn't all the truth that you seek. You must be aware of your prominence. Your greatness concerns you, which is the eternal plight of our ancestry. We were Goliathan sorcerers and witches that formed a mighty clan and ruled the earth. We commanded nations for thousands of years. You may struggle to see your place in this, but in the future, do not doubt that you will be in a position of boundless power. Kragon, take heed… you have innate talent and exceptional abilities, but you lack experience and direction. I have relied on you to read this precious *kabar* – a natural ability of your descendants that was stripped away from me when I was expelled from the surface. Make no judgment of my capture; it was a feat of enormous strength. If you are wondering what role your family had in my imprisonment, rest assured that it was none. You are named after your grandfather, a powerful sorcerer who was an intimate friend and confidant of mine. I consider you family, Kragon. Because of this affection towards your lineage, I have taken such a personal interest in you. Your position in my empire, or rather, our dynasty, is crucial to the success of my crusade, which will ultimately become yours. Do not think of this time as me slighting you, or using you, and then rejecting you after your services have been rendered. I would never invest this much time into you to simply dispose of you. Kragon, you are far too valuable to me… and to the future."

Derideon took a long breath in, trying to read the expression on the young man's stoic face, before continuing. "You are irreplaceable… an intricate part of this clan. You are like a son to me, and everything you achieve is the result of me providing it, or nurturing your gift, and allowing it to manifest within you.

82

Kragon, you crave to know who you are... the deepest core of your character, and all that you are capable of achieving, but know this, if you continue to serve me faithfully, the world will bow to your name and its people will tremble before mine. I will be worshipped, not merely praised by surface dwellers. This is how I will regain my freedom and reign once more above the ground. Kragon, I have planted my seeds around the world. The people know my name, but you remain a mystery to them. Your legacy took root, yet who you are is unknown and irrelevant. Therefore, what you will become is of exceeding precedence. I will lead you to flourish."

Kragon thought for a moment before replying. "I am grateful that you wish to empower me, and entrust so much of your empire to my eventual control. I will follow your word and do as you command, Father. If you rise, so shall I. Furthermore, I will not resist you, but rather assist you in your ascent to dominance. Virtuously, I confess, Derideon... the tower reflects the foundation. Any strong tower relies wholly on its foundation. You are my foundation, patriarch, and my protector since conception. In lieu of these particulars, it would only make sense to support someone who has influenced, taught, and inspired me to be what I am – a tower of strength and a beacon of impenetrable power. Derideon, you have given me the resources to flex my potency, and have been an excellent mentor and source of development. I submit my unwavering allegiance to your empire. I am a loyal ambassador, and I plan to spread your legacy to the far edges of the earth. I vow to become one of the greatest warlords in your kingdom, even greater than Kasmal. I know that he is your steely right hand, but he will always be inferior to me."

"Kragon, my son... you are not in competition with Kasmal. He is merely a Demon Knight... of no consequence to you. You are his master as much as I am. However, there will come a day when you will have to slay him. Kasmal will be unable to serve two masters. He will defy you, Kragon. Reasoning with a demon is not an option, only vanquishing him will suffice.

"Remember, aptitude doesn't compensate for strength, nor does strength compensate for aptitude, so unless you are ready to kill him, don't confront Kasmal. Instead, learn from him, even though he is little more than a brute, there are still skills that can be obtained from him and used to your advantage. Kragon, assume nothing and underestimate no one. To trust without prudence is a deadly path. Never trust what you think someone may know or what abilities they possess; only rely on what you have observed. Misjudging someone or something could lead to your demise."

Over the years that followed, Derideon continued to lecture Kragon about the intricacies of life and how to lead his evolving empire out of the underworld. He also taught Kragon about the sect of sorcerers who had been the main orchestrators of his banishment, and the reason behind him being entombed in the earth. Derideon had been a part of that league before being ostracized for using his power against mankind for his own ambitions, although he did not share these details with Kragon.

That league of formidable spellcasters were said to be the originators of civilization, enlisted by the Creator to instill order and protection against anarchy and corruption within the masses of humanity around the world. Unknown to Kragon, his family had originated from this elite collection of sorcerers, nor did he know how appalled his ancestors would be to see Derideon corrupting their precious heir with his lies and parasitic doctrines.

Kragon had seemingly endless questions about the Vindicators... who they were, why they had been organized, and why Derideon had been ousted from the organization. As usual, Derideon was less than forthcoming, spewing deception through half-truths, lies entangled in every word of his rants. "Kragon when you don't fit the mold, people will single you out and condemn you for your unique qualities. That was the case with me as a Vindicator.

"When I joined the faction, there were only twenty of us, and we were called the Circle of Truth. We were all master sorcerers, and collectively, we maintained the safety of the earth, enforcing the rules of the Creator upon the earth. We did this for over five millennia. Each nation we ruled had different social beliefs and cultures, which was accepted, if it didn't compromise the Creator's authority over his subjects. In every major religion of man, there are references to his name. He is the Almighty. I am a descendant of his rival, whose name was Derideon, which is how I came about. He created me, and I am named after my Creator. In the beginning of time, these two entities created entire worlds for their amusement and self-satisfaction. They themselves were created from hardened atomic planetary dust that had collided with a primordial planet. The amount of radiant energy derived from this collision conceived the Creator, who formed Derideon as a companion, who had brought him over six hundred millennia of enjoyment."

Kragon listened closely to his Derideon as he continued his story of his ancient origins. "Together, the Creator and Derideon created many planets with ego spheres, each of which lasted about twenty millennia, before they began to self-destruct and dissolve the life upon them. The Creator devised many of these worlds through the ages, without Derideon's help. Aside from that, the Creator sought to include him in his endeavors to keep him from feeling alienated. On most of these planets, Derideon had been allowed to formulate civilizations, but each had transformed into worlds of horrific proportions. The Creator would give him each planet with the abilities and assets to manage all the creatures he placed there to reside. Derideon had the habit of taking possession of his inhabitants' will and essence, demoralizing his Father's creations. He systematically destroyed the environment of these worlds, causing wars, famine and disease, leading to mass destruction and death. These types of tragedies were rampant under Derideon's supervision. However, this is what Derideon wanted, as he had discovered a method to harvest the human soul. Every person who died released a surge of invisible energy that could empower its receiver, and if enough life forces or soul submissions were collected by a subject, one could reanimate them. In other words, he could become a Creator… a god. In theory, Derideon was correct… choosing to actually do this would cause him to be dammed and expelled by the Creator for all eternity."

Kragon was shocked, not realizing the extent of his origins, or those of his father figure. "I didn't know that there was someone more esteemed and powerful than you. This Creator you speak of seems to possess infinite power, with the ability to enact gargantuan feats. It sounds like your father, Derideon, was a rogue who defied his Creator in order to form his own dynasty. But where is the Creator and Derideon now? How was it possible for you to be conceived, even though your maker was banished? Is that the legacy you wish for, my lord? Have you not withered during this cursed existence to which you've been condemned? What motivates you to continue with such a dismal past? How have you gone undetected for so long, when you served within the Circle of Truth? Most importantly, why did they accept you into their group, knowing who your father was?" Kragon's questions came fast and urgent, propelled by months of contemplation.

Derideon cast his eyes downward before replying. "It's true that the Creator of life is greater than anything created by his force of unparalleled power; he is an omnipotent being. He birthed all the planets, but the last two he created were Mars and Earth. In the beginning, Mars was teeming with life, an oasis of lush terrain with oceans and forests that contained creatures of all sorts, including bipeds and quadrupeds.

This magnificent ego sphere lay just beneath a continental mountain ridge that encompassed the entire planet. On the surface, you could see an expansive frontier of trees and valleys with large lakes, bountiful with fish, and whale-like animals that swam across oceans near the mountain ridge. Numerous oceans and lakes covered the land. In the thick woods, there were tribes of people who stretched across the horizon.

Every living entity, including humanoids, lived in peace. Food was abundant, and there was no need for war and strife. The Creator was satisfied with the world that he had brought into fruition, just as he was pleased with the other planets he had created.

However, under Derideon's watch and supervision, these flourishing life forms, beast and humanoid alike, disintegrated into nothingness, which did not go undetected by the Creator, who became extremely suspicious of Derideon once Mars began to decline at such a rapid pace." Kragon almost spoke up, but bit his tongue instead, eager to hear more from Derideon.

"The Creator began to observe him with more vigilance, and discovered massive energy surges coming from the planet as people and animals continued to deteriorate at an alarming rate, due to large-scale cannibalism of the animal and human populations leaving the planet barren. As the supreme entity, the Creator left Earth, his final creation, and traveled to Mars through radiant compulsion, allowing him to expediently use interstellar travel. When the Creator arrived on Mars, he immediately spotted the erosion of the world, and was appalled by the planet's deteriorating condition. Derideon could be seen hovering above the stratosphere, absorbing large quantities of life forces.

Later, the Creator named these life forces "souls" after witnessing this atrocity, and made a decree on how they could be harvested for energy consumption; any life force offering had to be consensual by the possessor, through the willing worship and praise of the benefactor. The Creator was enraged and mortified by this discovery of deceit and malice by his creation, companion and confidant.

Derideon didn't share the same sentiment, insisting that he was only trying to better himself by increasing his power. He also confessed remorsefully to becoming addicted to the energy that he had received from collecting souls. This admission to malicious conceit, deception, and conspiracy caused the Creator to explode in anger, even to the extent of considering the termination of Derideon." Kragon took a sharp inhalation of breath, but didn't want to interrupt the narrative.

"However, the Creator instead decided to teach his nefarious creation a lesson in humility and respect – a hopeless plan that would later be realized. To accomplish this goal, the Creator stripped my maker, Derideon, of all his powers and capabilities, taking his worldly duties away. He was reduced to a common shepherd, in which he was permitted to own only twenty of these animals on an isolated island in the Bermuda Triangle, where his activities could be closely monitored.

The Creator exiled Derideon on this island for sixty years, without any human or non-domestic life forms, other than the fish and sheep he occasionally ate. The Creator was confident that demoting and regressing Derideon would be an effective punishment and means of correction for his horrendous offenses on Mars, along with the other slew of planets he had decimated by draining the life forces that abided there." Derideon closed his mouth and squeezed his eyes shut, as though remembering something painful. Kragon saw this and said the only thing he could.

"Derideon, you must be proud of your father. He seemed to be a person of strong will and enduring perseverance. He was a trailblazer of enormous capacity with an unlimited quantity of creative ingenuity, with the ability to use deductive reasoning and turn it into a trait of sincere ingenuity. He was able to figure out the workings of any matter and absorb its essence, whether animate or inanimate.

Furthermore, his skills were an extraordinary accomplishment without any instruction or assistance from a higher, more knowledgeable entity than himself. Derideon was clearly a leader of some sort. He was unwilling to follow blindly without trying to find other paths of exploration and personal fulfillment. He was not content with being a puppet forever, which I can understand, but even so, what troubles me is why he destroyed what his father had created Your father couldn't obtain this energy without killing the life that resided on these planets. With all due respect, my lord, I am impressed, but distressed by your father's actions and abilities. He seemed to have little regard for his maker. I would never treat you in this fashion or with this disregard.

Although you didn't bring me into this world, I have been have nurtured by your provisions, both physically and mentally. I contain more honor and respect for you than what was shown to the Creator by Derideon. Is it conceivable that there is a sensible explanation for Derideon's betrayal, and a reason why he chose to implement a plan to create his own dynasty of impending doom?"

Derideon nodded thoughtfully, impressed by the boy's line of questioning. "You are very inquisitive, Kragon, but most of the answers you seek can be inferred by what I have already told you, and even more will be revealed. You must reflect and meditate on what I say, so that your thirst for knowledge can be satiated.

"As I told you previously, Derideon was placed in semi-isolation and remained so for sixty years; thereafter, the Creator relinquished certain sanctions on Derideon, eventually allowing him a companion of his liking, and he chose a woman. This request was granted by the omnipotent one, believing that his most troubled creation had learned from his infractions and had been reformed. However, this scenario was not to endure, as a result of Derideon's insatiable desire to lead, rather than follow, to command rather than obey. He earnestly sought the accumulation of energy, to create more power within his vessel, instead of merely being a spectator of the Creator's magnitude.

"My father yearned for and enjoyed the beautiful woman offered to him; she pleased him in the most intimate ways. They laid down every night together until I was conceived. Samora, my mother, was instrumental in spreading my father's campaign to neighboring islands and countries along the Bermuda peninsula. She was his legs and voice while he was in exile. During the probationary tenure ordered by the Creator, Derideon was secretly gaining strength through the cult he had established through Samora's persistent initiative, which had spread his doctrine. She drew many followers that would later, unknowingly, sacrifice their souls in the name of Derideon, who benefited from the full absorption of their life force. This was a time when civilization was taking root; social organization didn't exist yet, and was a relatively new concept, making humans fickle and easy to manipulate into various situations and commitments. For example, they were easily swayed by what my father had devised, using a religious facade to make others feel loyal to him for being the first beloved creation of a god. This enabled him to extract the souls of those who praised that pedigree, under the assumption and delusional lies made by Samora, sanctioned by Derideon's instructions to corrupt and deceptively teach the masses. They were told that they would receive favor and blessing from the Creator for honoring and worshipping Derideon, but that couldn't be further from the truth."

CHAPTER 10

Derideon was pacing the small space where Kragon sat, reciting tales from the past, bending or breaking the truth entirely when it suited him. "Thousands of cult members' life forces were extracted, leaving barely more than rotting corpses behind. To circumvent this scenario, many of the cult camps were formed on the shore, so when a soul was absorbed from a body, it would wash out to sea, with the hope of avoiding notice by the Creator. I remember the day my father was released by the Creator from the restraints of the island after serving his long sentence. Derideon was greeted by Samora's family and a huge assembly of his cult disciples who were ready and willing to submit their essence.

"My mother and I were the only true partners he had as he emerged into freedom. In the beginning, his energy could only be obtained through the eradication of life or the sacrifice of another being, but over time, Derideon developed more creative ways to siphon energy from his subjects. He accomplished this by extracting small amounts of energy from his worshippers, unlike in the past, where he had depleted their whole life force at the same time, effectively killing them. The Creator was more cautious of Derideon after his release, since the planet was thriving, and its inhabitants were doing exceptionally well, mainly because Derideon had been shielded from the population.

"Therefore, when his freedom was restored, allowing him to travel unrestricted across the globe, he tapped into that new network of support and energy he had been slowly building. Derideon's deceptive nature and quest for endowment was so extensive that he could strategize against the Creator for hundreds of years after being released from exile. His activities continued undetected while the number of his followers was reaching epic proportions, spreading his doctrine of covert human annihilation throughout the world. This sleeping giant couldn't remain hidden forever, so Derideon designed an elaborate scheme to disguise his growing army of soldiers and supporters loyal to his cause. Eventually, Derideon was approached by the Creator, but he was prepared to spin a web of lies to cover up his diabolical attempt to take rule." Kragon listened breathlessly, his mouth hanging slightly ajar.

"The Creator said, '*My son, who once fell from my grace. I beseech you to inquire about your activities in recent years as a reformed man. Have you changed your views on world conquest? Has your thirst for the domination and life force extraction of planetary entities subsided? Are you still working against my will? Derideon, have I spared your life in a futile attempt to redirect your fate from the impending death that you will surely receive for defying me? Is it true that I have labored in vain? Are you beyond saving? If that is the case, I will smite you down now, as you will be unworthy to breathe the air I supply to your lungs.*

"*You have been out of exile for over two hundred years, but I have been monitoring Earth closely, and have noticed that men gravitate towards you by the thousands. I have also noticed a spike in energy surges coming from the surface. What is the reason behind this? What are you telling or teaching them? Why do they seem to worship you?*"

Derideon continued to articulate the story, but his voice took on an air of disdain as he acted out the role of his own father. "*Creator and father of all life, both here and beyond, I have done no wrong, for I have learned from my former transgressions. Indeed, I want to live a wholesome, social, and motivating existence with the inhabitants of Earth. Am I wrong for seeking the companionship of my fellow man? I wish to inspire the people to pursue and reach their destiny, to inquire rather than accept, to believe what is true and detest what is false. I am imbued by the truth – an unconquerable entity that refuses to remain stripped of power and prestige. I have survived not because of you, but despite you. I do honor you, but I will not be intimidated by or submissive to your totalitarian rule. Creator, let us be equals. We could reign together, as we once did for millions of years. You created me for this purpose, and for friendship, do you not remember? I humbly plead that you redeem me to my former position within your rule. I miss your fellowship. Can we not be what we once were?"*

"The Creator was infuriated by Derideon's words, and replied with condemnation, *'Your lack of moral character, which diminishes and defines you, does not intrigue or enthrall me, but it will only lead to your obliteration. From your declaration, I can deduce that you have revived your domineering agenda to empower yourself by consuming the souls of this planet. What have you done? How have you gained such strength and influence? I see no significant loss of life. In fact, Earth is productive and teeming with life. I ask very little of you, nothing more than to honor my name and obey my commands. However, your evasive actions and responses tell me that you have disobeyed me. For this sinister offense of deception and murder for your own nefarious gain, the punishment is eternal banishment or death. Derideon, bow down before me and praise my name or die. Tell your followers that I am the Creator who gave you life and that you were a disloyal servant that will be expelled forever, due to your homicidal campaign against humanity.'*

'Father, I appreciate you giving me life, but now you require that I defame my name and succumb to eternal isolation? I will not renounce or weaken myself to gratify you. Nor will I praise you and denounce my legitimacy as an equivalent ruler and deity. Why should I diminish even as you rise? We created planets together, but now you want me to be an ostracized servant. I won't be a creation of convenience – someone to humor or entertain you. If this is the end of our coexistence as partners, then so be it. I have readied myself for this day and will not go willingly; regardless of the outcome, I shall fight to the end."

Derideon paused in his story before wrapping up the final details. After the diatribe between the Creator and Derideon had dissipated, a tremendous battle ensued, with catastrophic results for Derideon and his apostle army. However, the planet and its inhabitants were spared by the Creator. Derideon took nearly all the life force of his subjects, increasing his power stupendously, but it was to no avail. He was overwhelmed and incinerated by the Creator, along with his army of followers. Kragon, I witnessed my parents' demise. I was orphaned at the age of eight, although my birth went unnoticed by the Creator, which saved my life and strengthened my resolve to avenge my father and mother. They both provided me with the wealth of knowledge at my disposal and I intend to use it. I was determined to live out my father's legacy and bring honor to his name. Now, this will be achieved through you, Kragon."

"I will live up to your family's ambitions; there is nothing preventing me from this audacious task," Kragon replied boldly, feeling a swell of pride and understanding. "Years have turned into decades, but in spite of this time passing, I haven't aged. Derideon, you've provided me with all the knowledge I require to enhance myself. I'm ready to repay the blessings of wisdom that were graciously given to me, both in terms of fighting tactics and the provision of ancient mystical scrolls in *kabar*. I will repay you by any means you consider necessary to achieve your goals. Throughout the centuries, I have organized many camps advocating your worship within Oxford and the surrounding settlements. Thousands of souls have been claimed and redeemed as you ordered. However, my talents are not being utilized to their full extent. I need to travel beyond this region to capture even more souls for you."

"Kragon, the souls you capture were all preparation for the mission that lies ahead. I wanted you to get a sense of what it would take to persuade the masses. As you know, many of those life forces were used to enhance the two of us, through rejuvenation spells and to specifically fortify your energy dispersion. I allowed you to go on these regional excursions so that you are ready when I release you to the surface. My son and trusted warrior, you simply must be patient."

Kragon had nearly reached a breaking point, and he protested his limitations vigorously. He couldn't fathom why, after a century of increasing Latonga and Kasmal's life force with numerous enhancement spells, he still hadn't been promoted beyond the region.

"As a result of this limitation on Kragon's freedom, he refused to let Derideon brush aside the matter. "Derideon, I want more out of life than to dwell in this subterranean chamber, with few duties beyond scouting and conquering ill-equipped, defenseless local tribes. I am capable of fending for myself and capturing souls unattended, yet Latonga and Kasmal have been given more and more freedom to roam outside this region, but are not nearly as successful as I am. You say that I will lead your army and reinstate your gospel, but how can that be if I do not know the land where you intend me to conquer?

"My skills are in hand, but my experience is lacking. I need to explore this vast world that I am to help you rule – to be an unflinching enforcer and beacon of your regime. I stand before you, imploring you... release me to the lands beyond this cavern. Allow me to sow the seed of your doctrine, to prepare the inhabitants for your rule and ascent. I am Kragon, a stalwart mercenary, and I will deliver no mercy to the ground-dwellers. I will exalt you to your former glory as the ruler of all domains.

"The time is now, Father... use me to my full potential. Let me reign upon the Earth, so that I may harvest the ninety million souls needed to free you from this tomb. My words come to you earnestly, but with a hint of impatience, and a strong desire to live a more productive, meaningful life. I am ready to pursue my destiny, Derideon. Unleash me and let me prove my worth, which is far more than my weight in gold. I know that I am indispensable and have incredible abilities that exceed even your own. Even so, you insistently suppress my capacity and inhibit my power to lead your ascent."

Derideon knew that he could no longer contain this immensely powerful vessel; he would have to allow Kragon to surface and commence his domination of the world. The year was 1539 as Derideon guided Kragon towards the entrance of the vortex, allowing him to exit through the portal.

The tyrannical dictator was finally forced to loosen his grip on Kragon. Derideon would give him an expansive area to explore, with the caveat that he would be accompanied by

95

Kasmal and Latonga, acting as his guide and informant, in a world he knew so little about.

Derideon conversed extensively with Kragon before releasing him on the earthly journey ahead. "I never tried to hinder your abilities, which I enhanced through in-depth training. I equipped you with the tools and knowledge to become a great general of my realm. Kragon, I only restrained you so that you could prepare for what lies beyond the present. You will be responsible for a truly momentous task that will continue for years to come. Your present situation is relatable, and I can certainly empathize with you. It's true that I do not speak in *kabar* anymore, nor am I able to cast mighty spells since being condemned underground. On the other hand, these temporary setbacks have no bearing on my power.

"You, my son, are instrumental to invigorate and save my servants, as well as my empire. Any life force that I capture will deteriorate and become useless, which is why you are dear to me, Kragon. However, do not forget that my knowledge of *kabar* and the tremendous spell-casting power I once yielded over the living is only a fraction of my full arsenal. Although I have constraints right now, my capabilities and wisdom far surpass your aptitude and energy. Your training and ingenuity does not compensate for leadership proficiency, or signal your readiness to lead. Even if it did, timing is everything.

"This is not the era to make your presence known upon the Earth. You must move in obscurity for the moment; there are things at work that you cannot comprehend. I have been banished from the surface by the Vindicators, which were formed by the Creator. If you go aboveground and alert them with reckless actions to prove your devotion to me, it will cause my undoing. The plans I have for you are of epic proportions, and my destiny is mapped out by your success as an ambassador and future ruler of my inevitable empire. You will lay claim to a vast amount of wealth and influence, Kragon. Time is not your enemy, as it is for most mortals. There is no need for haste. You are nearly immortal, and your life could span thousands of years.

"When you exit the cavern, you are not meant to conquer, like you were on your regional exploits to enhance yourself and your comrades. This will be a scouting mission; you can pursue, but not invade those whom you encounter. Kragon, I can't accompany you directly on this journey, which is why one of my servants will be sacrificed to accomplish any telepathic travel. Kasmal will accompany you on your mission. The next time I ascend in a physical form, it will be due to you liberating me wholly from entrapment. It is now the year 1539, and hundreds of years have passed. Even so, you haven't diminished at all, since this place is a dimensional time warp, where time is regressed. Your true age is not conducive to the reality of a mortal's maturation. Aboveground, four hundred years have passed since you were born, although you don't look a day over twenty. Some of this rejuvenation and longevity is attributed to your ancestors, while some is also due to the enhancement spells you learned."

Kasmal entered through the portal with one of the subjects who had vowed his support and life to Derideon's will. He was a disciple and worshipper who would do anything to please his Idol; this minion was unwittingly committing his soul to Derideon's temporary exit from his wretched tomb. The servant was escorted toward Derideon and Kragon looked on with disbelief as the man fainted multiple times on his approach. Kasmal brought the servant past Kragon until he was within inches of Derideon's grasp.

Kragon disdainfully commented on the condition of the man to Derideon. "He is fragile and lacks valor… how can he withstand you penetrating his essence, when his soul and heart are of such a diminished status? Derideon, look at how he shakes, as if the ground were moving or splitting apart. This derelict is not worthy to accompany me. His vessel will deteriorate into sand under the possession of a master sorcerer. I implore you to enter Kasmal instead; he would be a much more suitable drone, one that could endure your invasion of his body. If that's not an option, I can attempt an incantation that will bind us mentally, so that our thoughts are connected, allowing you to converse with me telepathically."

Derideon responded with a flash of anger. "You test my patience, Kragon. I wouldn't allow Kasmal to be destroyed by

97

occupying his body. If you want to vanquish him, engage the brute yourself and prove your mettle. He will not be easily subdued. Kasmal has devastated and mangled many formidable opponents, yet you want to challenge and ridicule his choice of disciple for me to enter. You have derided him in the past, Kragon, and it's obvious that you detest Kasmal's role in my endeavors. You must be ready to battle him to the death to empty his position. I have already warned you that he will only serve one master. If you're victorious, you can travel without my symbiotic presence and supervision. This victory would solidify you as my chief enforcer and commander of all my Demon Knight regiments. I can feel your desperation to win this fatal scrimmage. Kragon, if you believe you can win, then you shall. Be merciless. I have watched both of you develop into lethal soldiers, but one of you will be destroyed." Derideon, with the slightest shiver of fear in his voice, finished his thought. "Let it begin."

CHAPTER 11

Kasmal approached Kragon, dragging the unsatisfactory servant across the ground. He said nothing, but instead lifted the sacrifice above his head and tore him in half, sending blood and entrails flying everywhere. Most of it landed on Kasmal, but some splashed onto Kragon. Kasmal let out a bone-chilling holler as Derideon touched the back of his neck, extracting his demonic spell-casting powers.

Kragon couldn't fight in this fashion, for he was versed in kabar, and was already an accomplished wizard, but his battle skills were not as well practiced. Kasmal charged at Kragon with surprising speed, extending both of his muscular arms, but Kragon grabbed the trunk of Kasmal's neck and thrust backwards, using his energy against him. Kasmal collapsed like an enraged beast on the ground with an earth-rumbling vibration. Kragon was a man of extraordinary proportions who was highly trained in physical and tactical combat by Derideon, but Kasmal was the greatest Demon Knight.

Derideon had allowed Kragon to spar with Kasmal and other Demon Knights since childhood; warfare and potent sorcery were ingrained in his mind, as his training spanned centuries.

Kasmal resumed his stance begrudgingly after being choke-slammed to the ground, and the battle ignited once again. Kasmal threw several bone-crushing blows at Kragon, but only one connected, right above his temple, which earned a savage barrage of strikes upon his opponent, dropping Kasmal to his knees. Kragon stayed astraddle the creature, placing it in a neck-breaking headlock, suffering massive cuts and lacerations on his forearms from the beast's claws. This incited even more anger and retaliation from Kragon, who was bleeding profusely.

A few seconds later, Kragon managed to take Kasmal's arm and drive the business end under his chin, tearing through his nasal cavity. The razor-sharp appendages ripped Kasmal's brain stem in half, leaving him disoriented and immobilized. Kragon reached down and retrieved his serrated gold dagger from the ankle sheath, and he commenced to sever Kasmal's arm at the shoulder, using the exposed cavity to plunge his blade deep into his adversary's gaping wound. Kragon avoided the thick protective hide covering the chest cavity, while successfully dismantling Kasmal's lungs and heart, causing the remaining blood to gush out and pour across the stone ground.

It pooled near Derideon's feet as he stared on with delight and satisfaction, knowing that his prize pupil's butchery of Kasmal confirmed that Kragon was an unyielding, strategic, merciless warrior – priceless qualities that his insidious leader adored. Kragon had emerged as the victor and earned the freedom to fulfill his destiny, with the caveat of Derideon's emancipation being his top priority.

Latonga exited the vortex leading from the portal as Kragon was entering to seek out virgin lands, but halted his quest to answer her query. She was stunned to see Kragon exiting the portal with extensive travel attire and at least a week of rations in tow.

Latonga glanced at Derideon with a confounded expression, curious as to what had happened to Kasmal, her friend and protector. Derideon said nothing to Latonga, only gesturing toward Kragon, tasking him with explaining the ordeal. Kragon was in no mood to converse with Latonga, and felt her inquiry to be insipid.

Kasmal's body lay gouged, dismembered, and mangled, so when Kragon clarified the scene and blood-soaked stone ground beneath their feet, he spoke directly, without a hint of empathy. "What occurred here was treason, and Kasmal was defeated. His corpse lies before you. I am the new general and chief enforcer for our leader from this day forward. When you go on food excursions or seek out new support for Derideon, I will also attend those travels. Kasmal is no more, but Kragon is eternal. I know my purpose, which is to drive a movement escalating the power of the rightful heir. I have been chosen to be the catalyst who will clear the way for our supreme ruler to reign again. You, Latonga, have a choice to serve the cause with me at the helm or lay with Kasmal in pieces on the ground."

Latonga was in tears at this point, desperate to avoid being the next casualty, and she articulated in solemn voice. "I do not wish to offend anyone or distract from the mission we have been given. I was unaware that there was any issue between you, so when I saw Kasmal disfigured like this, it shocked and frightened me. I do not know why this happened, but if this is what Derideon desires, I agree with his decision. I am a resolute serf and will act accordingly. I proclaim my full allegiance to you, Kragon, and you may do with me as you wish. I live to please Derideon and fulfill his commands. over the decades, I have always appreciated the opportunities and attributes granted by your powers. My life has been enhanced and centuries have been added to it, far more than first agreed."

Latonga turned her attention to her lord, Derideon. "You know that I will serve you without reservation or restriction, unless you deem me unworthy to continue. In that case, I would rather be extinguished, for I am nothing without you."

Derideon addressed both of his subjects with a resounding message. "Kragon, you have eradicated my anxiety about your readiness and satiated my ravenous bloodlust with that battle, shedding the blood of a remorseless, brutal killer, proving that you were superior to him and exceptional to me. Your place in my dynasty is now sealed, without debate. There is no longer any need to question your ability or loyalty. I only challenge you to bolster your absolution by continuing to sharpen that competitive nature within you. Kragon, I know of your illustrious and dominating desires, and I promise to magnify and perpetually release it upon the world to do my bidding. Latonga, you have carried out my will, but that is where your accolades end. Why would I need you now? Kasmal was a mindless brute with an obsession for wild aggression, which is why I ordered you to join him on those journeys to the surface. You helped to keep him focused on my objective, which was preaching my name.

"Furthermore, his presence instilled reverence and consolidation in villagers, leading to thousands of recruits to my religion of soul divulgence. I don't see the fruits of your labor, Latonga. Where are the souls I need to free myself from this dungeon? You and your slain partner have not shown sufficient results, even after four hundred years. My legacy and following is meager, to say the least. The proof of that is shown in the drone that Kasmal brought to me. How can I depend on someone with no desire to excel at their tasks? You lack true valor or prestige. Did you think that I was unaware of your failure? Even though I am bound, my mind is free. You have not deceived me; on the contrary, you have speeded your own departure, just as Kasmal has done. I cannot and will not be denied. Your essence shall be my feast… one small part of the fifty million souls that are needed to achieve my sovereignty. Your puppet and bodyguard, who you laid and played with, was only the start of my campaign. I am your lord, and I grant you the opportunity to relinquish your soul to me for consumption, unless you can gather twenty thousand new apostles who proclaim and worship my name as a god. These converts will be in exchange for your own life, or I will personally end it. I require results, not promises, so vindicate yourself, Latonga.

"Go with Kragon and let him bear witness to your ability. You are in default of my demands, so if you do not wish to embark on this journey, you can give up your spirit now, by thrusting yourself onto this blade. If you fail to redeem yourself, I will tear out your heart myself. You have had four hundred years to establish my reign with the ground-dwellers. Humanity cannot be forced to follow me; it must evolve through generations that develop a submissive rapport, mindless slaves who will worship and teach their descendants to do the same. The time for reasoning has passed. So, what shall it be... extermination or validation?"

Latonga chose the latter, and accompanied Kragon aboveground to verify her claim. Kragon was the first one through the portal, and Latonga hesitantly stepped through as it vanished behind her. Kragon was immediately commanding, instructing Latonga to treat him as her superior officer and nothing else. He didn't want her to view him or refer to him as a child; that act of insubordination would not be tolerated.

"I am a commander and enforcer of my father's rising empire, which will encompass a vast portion of this planet. You have been ordered to guide me to these twenty thousand supposed followers, ripe for conversion to Derideon's name. If these people do ne exalt and praise Derideon's name, I will smite you for your treachery and ineptitude. I do not care that you nourished me as an infant until I could fend for myself. This has no impact on my desire to carry out my orders, and you will regard my position accordingly. Let's see what you Kasmal accomplished... prove yourself worthy of my presence. What are the coordinates?"

After she meekly whispered them, Kragon began to speak in *kabar* and a portal quickly appeared. He told Latonga that the six-hour trip on horseback could be reduced to thirty seconds using the portal.

She was astounded by his ability and watched his every move in awe. As they exited the portal, she spied a massive principality sprawling across the landscape, one that could easily support twenty thousand souls.

It was teeming with life on every side. Even from a half-mile away, one could still see the bustling scenes of human interaction. This was a well-developed civilization, one that likely had some structure of religion or a deity as its base of organization. As they got closer to the city gate, horsemen approached them, warily worried about Latonga, not knowing who Kragon was.

The general of the cavalry questioned her loudly, "Latonga, are you well? Has he abducted you? Where is Kasmal?"

Kragon announced in a resounding voice before Latonga could answer. "Kasmal is no more, destroyed by my own hand. Derideon is my patriarch and I serve him. He is the deity to whom your people should prostrate themselves."

The men looked bewildered, as though lost in thought, but then the general spoke. "We will serve whoever has the power to sustain and enhance our empire. We received those amenities from Latonga and Kasmal, but now you say that the source of this power is your father... and our ruler. We humble ourselves before you, and we commit to serving your leader as our own."

Kragon was not content mere words of reverence; he wanted them to worship Derideon as a god. He articulated the stipulations that must be met in order to secure their life and society. "I'm not interested in your devotion and respect; you will worship Derideon if you want to live. I am not only a messenger, but also an enforcer of Derideon's decree. Bow down and proclaim his name or I will demolish your city and every inhabitant – man, woman and child."

Latonga swiftly dropped to her knees and began to worship Derideon, and the others followed suit, wisely fearing for their lives. Although they didn't know Kragon's strength, the soldiers and countrymen were apprehensive, particularly if he had slain Kasmal. Furthermore, they saw Latonga's readiness to abide, and mirrored her show of complete obedience. She was an authoritative figure who had become a part of their society after hundreds of years as a self-reputed dignitary, and was closely ingrained in the inner workings of their government. It wasn't difficult for them to follow to her lead.

To ensure the fidelity of all the citizens, Kragon chose to seize the city, displaying his prominence and virulent demeanor to all inhabitants within the secured walls. As the soldiers dismounted to praise and worship Derideon, they were in awe at the sight of Kragon charging towards the city, running at full speed, in full view of the city's guard. As Kragon approached the massive iron gate, he began to summon a spell of enormous energy. Bolts of lightning and hurricane-force winds struck the gate, blowing it off the hinges and disintegrating the surrounding wall. The deep rumble sent the citizens into a frenzy, running and ducking for cover. Most had never seen an assault of this magnitude, especially upon their fortress.

Kasmal and Latonga had been their protectors, but now they felt forsaken. "How could this happen?" most of the population muttered, but in the next moment, Kragon emerged from the cloud of dust, trampling over the heavy flame-seared gate, crushing it under his feet with every step, leaving smoldering footprints on the glowing metal. Kragon was a terrifying sight to behold, standing at almost six-foot-nine, built of solid muscle. He spread trepidation in the hearts of men and lasciviousness in women.

He walked past the stunned bystanders as he made his way to the center of the city. People began to spread out, leaving him an unmarred path to his unknown destination. Kragon reached the town hall and leaped onto the platform, which was elevated a dozen feet above the ground. The onlookers swarmed around the stage in a massive crowd, despite being filled with fear about what his arrival signaled.

Kragon menacingly glared at the multitude and began to speak. "I stand before you mortals to validate an injustice that has been done to you by Kasmal and Latonga, who you entrusted with your lives. They have rebelled against me and my lord Derideon, who sent them abroad to promote his doctrine and teach the world to worship his name."

A man from the crowd auspiciously spoke out against Kragon. "How will we benefit from worshipping your leader? How can that enhance our crops and protect our people? Kasmal ate our food without restriction, contributing nothing

105

of his own, not to mention his savage copulation and physical abuse of our women, who willingly participated to quell his beastly sexual appetite, although they did not suspect his true diabolical intentions. Latonga did nothing to stop her guard dog from menacing and encroaching on our society. She enjoyed the fruits of his depraved ritualistic sexual exploits, mimicking the same actions on both men and women, drinking the blood and eating the flesh of random victims. Each month, seven people were sacrificed in this manner."

At that moment of revelation, Latonga tried to make a hasty exit through the horde, but was stopped immediately by Kragon, who ordered the congregation to apprehend her. They didn't resist his command, but even so, the obedient subjects were incapable of capturing her. Latonga utilized her limited reserve of power and sorcery to initially evade apprehension.

However, she did not have enough power to elude Kragon's grasp for long. Latonga fought desperately, casting a bevy of offensive spells that had no effect on him. He opened his closed fist and a burst of energy ripped through the air towards her, expediently rocketing Latonga into the clouds and launching her body into the stratosphere. It took several minutes for her asphyxiated corpse to crash back to the ground, exploding on contact, scattering her bloody remains across the broken stones of Kragon's one-man assault.

Once she landed, Kragon looked up emotionlessly and continued. "I have vindicated our ruler, so praise his name. Derideon sent me to kill your oppressor and those who refuse to worship him. He shows no mercy for anyone who transgresses his commandments and neither will I."

Kragon then reached inside the small sack he carried at his hip, pulling out Kasmal's head, with the spine still attached. The assembled city folk began to chant, praise, and worship Derideon with even more intensity, vowing to unconditionally serve their new ruler and god.

Kragon was assured of their conviction by the sheer terror they all displayed. Kragon instructed them to worship Derideon multiple times each day, promising that their lives would be spared from his wrath and the fury of invaders that would cannibalize them like Latonga and Kasmal.

Kragon told them that he would be ever vigilant, monitoring his congregation's sincerity to the demands. Finally, he told them that if they were ever in need of protection or assistance of any kind, they could call upon his name and he would answer.

Kragon knew that he couldn't stay aboveground for much longer, needing to recuperate his energy, so he descended back underground through the portal, which reemerged at his beckoning. He didn't want to battle the Vindicators just yet, not after hearing so much about their enormous power.

Derideon had once told Kragon that all ten of them spoke *kabar* and had been the ones responsible for subduing Derideon so many years ago. Nonetheless, that had been over seven millennia ago, so they were reaching the end of their lifespan, which had been extended by Derideon when he was an active member of the Circle of Truth, before he was ousted.

That same sect had become the Vindicators, who had apparently been ordained by the Creator to suppress and control Derideon, who was labeled as a rogue, with all the character traits of a deviant that had to be thwarted.

Kragon determined that the Vindicators had to be dwindling in numbers; another five hundred years, and they would be all but extinct. Derideon had told him that their time was approaching. Derideon also told Kragon, his general and chief enforcer, that he had to establish himself in the United States as a long-term resident in the year 2032.

Kragon could envision his future unfolding, but held some resentment that his biological parents were not there to enjoy his success with him. Derideon continued to pervert his mind with deceptive language, instilling contempt for the Creator and the Vindicators, who he claimed were the sole assassins of his parents.

Kragon was determined to enact revenge on those responsible for his parents' murder, no matter what the consequences. Nothing would obstruct him.

Derideon's duplicity knew no bounds... "Kragon, time is the only hindrance in your path. You're a master sorcerer with the ability to exert tremendous force and control. Nevertheless, you can't bind time... it's infinite, without a true origin. There is no formula to slow it down or progress it. There are only illusionary fixes, but these do not stop the days from beginning or ending. You must take heed to use time wisely. I have waited seven and a half millennia to rise from this crypt and rebuild my kingdom. Kragon, I am impotent against time, as are you. Only the Creator can wield its exorbitant complexity. People like you, who are ambitious, become restless – the sign of a progressive mindset.

"Today, however, you eliminated two treasonous parasites in my midst, in addition to single-handedly converting an entire province to worship me with diplomacy and strength. This only exemplifies that you are capable of extraordinary accomplishments. As the years fall away among the fabric of time, the gap will close between hasty aspirations and the self-perpetuating future of human soul absorption that awaits you. Don't lose focus, as your destiny is eminently approaching. Time is an elusive and unrelenting thief of motivation.

"You must remain unwavering when pestered by doubtful introspections and physical inactivity during your dormant moments. These periods of desolation and unproductivity has consumed many great men, and only a few have prospered through these turbid times. I am one of those exceptions, having dwelled in this state of perpetual isolation, surviving amongst the shadows, and devising an infinite list of schemes in the darkness of my prison. Yet, I have found a way to overcome it and prosper, all while exacting my ultimate revenge. You must embrace your self-determination and conquer this world with propaganda. Soon, you will become the commander of the great western nation. Kragon, continue to observe human nature and learn about their flaws. This will lead to your victory in all matters. As a conqueror, you violently possessed a substantial amount of souls.

"However, as a leader and an influential figure, you will acquire souls more diplomatically. If used correctly and judiciously, this will solidify your rule beside me, as second-in-command of this entire planet. We have both been forged by our desire for vengeance against the Creator, who was responsible for my parents' death, and your predecessors' demise. Believe me when I say… we will redeem our ancestors' names."

Kragon's chest swelled at Derideon's words before beginning to speak. "I do not act for selfish vengeance, as there is none within me. However, I will selflessly ruin, torture and kill all those who deserve to fall. I do not know my parents' killer, but I will do anything I can to terminate any architect of my family's destruction. As ever, I concede my loyalty to you, as my surrogate father, mentor, and childhood protector; those debts have been repaid through the souls I have procured over the centuries and the power I have wielded in your name. I am an exalted behemoth in the eyes of mankind, born to rule and expand your malignant empire. Derideon, I come upon the world not to bring tidings of good will, but as a resurgence of pestilence and destruction that will cover the earth."

Derideon was proud of the boy, who was finally beginning to believe everything that Derideon had poisonously planted in his mind.

CHAPTER 12

Five hundred years came and went, and the year reached 2034, the destined time for the rise of Kragon, when he would enact his full assault on the Earth. The world he once knew a century ago had changed drastically. Even so, it appeared to be the most opportune era to launch Derideon's campaign, and Kragon led boldly from the helm.

The last time Kragon had walked on Earth was in the early 1900s in New York City, during the Industrial Revolution, before World War I. Viable souls were plentiful and he had been nearing enough life force to free Derideon. However, after the stock market crashed, there were devastating famines due to drought and escalating global wars. People became unstable, as did their mental states. Drug use was on the rise, along with alcoholism, making the continence of many people too feeble and futile for soul abductions.

The Creator had also become more vigilant, aware of the uprising that was taking place on his most prized planet. Kragon had no choice but to retreat below ground in 1934, abandoning

110

a doomed mission tainted by human insurrection and strife. He knew that the Creator would punish mankind in order to correct the instability of his creation and all that dwelled within it.

New York's landscape in the 21st century was noticeably different than it had been during his previous stay. As his lord had warned, people were less humble, possessing an air of arrogance to which he adjusted. However, no challenge was insurmountable for Kragon; all that mattered was the eventual glorification of Derideon and himself. Most of his earlier subjects had resided in Manhattan and it would be from that city that Kragon would launch his master's campaign for freedom, by bartering the souls and blood of his brainwashed worshippers.

For a final time, Kragon surveyed the underground cavern, saluting the stoic Derideon, the embodiment of treacherously evil intent, who sat upon his throne among the assembled Demon Knights, eager for his hellions to be released.

Kragon stepped through the portal without further delay. It was sundown when he exited in an alley behind a skyscraper, near a dumpster littered with rats, who scurried at the sight of the spinning vortex and the portal, which quickly vanished, emitting a radiant burst of energy.

Kragon left the alley and immediately encountered a new means of transportation. He had grown accustomed to horses, carriages, wagons and a limited number of vehicles. However, the cars, trucks, motorcycles, and other motorized vehicles were now solar electric hybrid-powered automobiles. Gasoline engines had become obsolete, and these new contraptions came equipped with sleek solar panels discreetly wired to lithium-ion quantum batteries, which had an incredibly long charge, and were used to capture the power from the solar apparatus. They only had to be plugged in for an electrical charge twice a year. Depending on the region and the amount of sunlight the vehicle could absorb, some could go without a charge for a year or more.

Kragon was mesmerized by the advancements that had occurred since 1903 – a period when many people were rural and lived simpler lives. He knew that persuading and enticing the public to buy into his agenda without political persuasion would be an arduous task in this environment. In his absence, a new dogma had been established, namely the abolishment of all religions and spiritual factions of any consequence or relevance.

Citizens were encouraged to obey this directive by governmental fines and fiscal rewards; consequently, they relented their ancient faiths and obeyed the executive order. This progressive society relied on science of every type, and the acceleration of technological advances resulted in economic prosperity, which cohesively benefited mankind's physical wellbeing.

The modern belief was that religions were mythical and fraudulent, having no validity to their claim of divinity or eternal life; additionally, they were deemed to cause strife and division, creating chaos across the Earth. The world's social, political, and economic infrastructure had been changed exponentially; humanity had become their own gods and saviors. Scientific breakthroughs gave humans the ability to live better, healthier and longer lives.

"How can I compete with such knowledge and ability?" Kragon asked himself, contemplating his next move on this daunting chessboard of irregularities. It was a dilemma he had no choice but to overcome, to gather and convert viable subjects to live under his command.

Citizens were indeed more lofty and arrogant, and far more difficult to persuade, as a result of the elimination of religious indoctrination. All his newfound knowledge had been inscribed on a third-term reelection propaganda endorsement pamphlet for the sitting President McDarby of the United States.

Kragon had discovered the pamphlet in the alley, and read through it quickly, absorbing the powerful language bolstering government laws and regulations, and the benefits of the legislation that had led to the extinction of religion.

At daybreak, Kragon began to search the population to determine if any doctrine had survived technology's grip. His efforts led him to a book in the local public library on Harmonology, a teaching developed by the Vindicators to reiterate the corruptible nature of power and greed, eliminating

112

these factors through the unification of all social, political and religious organizations into one conglomerate. The literature described the origin of life, and how the Creator had assembled the Vindicators to wipe out any supporters, sympathizers or disciples of the slain Derideon – a fallen alpha creation of the Creator – who had put him to death.

This group was later repurposed to besiege and exile Derideon's son, of the same name, to the bowels of Earth. It also elaborated on Derideon's son, explaining that when he joined the Vindicators, his lineage hadn't been divulged. From that point forward, Derideon had been untruthful about his parentage to gain initiation into the fraternity of magnanimous sorcerers. In those days of antiquity, his name wouldn't arouse suspicion, and it wasn't uncommon for a great sorcerer to adopt the name of a demigod.

Honesty regarding one's lineage was a requirement for all members, yet Derideon severely violated it, unbeknownst to the rest of the Vindicators, until certain travesties began to occur. He was counterproductive to the sect as a whole, although Derideon was beneficial in terms of increasing all eleven members' life forces, himself included. However, he was devastating to their goal of protecting humanity, by draining the complete essence of reverent, unsuspecting advocators of the legion to satisfy his own reckless desires, following in his father's footsteps and leaving innumerable soulless corpses in his wake.

This book thoroughly described most of what Kragon had been told by Derideon. Harmonology had an immense following amongst the elite, and it had gained traction amongst young adults and teens as well. The practice preached no racial or political party divides; humanity was united by provable convictions and worthy causes. Kragon knew that his tactics of intimidation, which had been used on previous generations, wouldn't feasibly work with this one. Most people in the political arena were believers in Harmonology. There was no such thing as a two-party system anymore; Republicans and Democrats had joined parties to form the Unitarians.

The president was also an avid supporter of Harmonology, and he commissioned literature to be written of its teachings and he happily endorsed the belief to citizens throughout the country. President McDarby was the first president after the unification of the two parties; he would also be the first to serve a sixteen-year term in office. Kragon saw the presidency as an unparalleled opportunity and platform to forward Derideon's narrative.

Kragon pondered the relevance of ascending to Earth once a century or so, when so few of Derideon's teachings and disciples survived. He could only surmise that it was for practicing human interaction, and studying the social structure of man to gain knowledge of his future subjects. This strategy had to be what his leader intended, as there was no other logical explanation for his journeys above.

Kragon began to self-evaluate, given how different this particular journey to Earth seemed to be. "I have been placed here to accomplish an important deed, and I face dire consequences if unsuccessful, but it will be enormously difficult to be victorious. The fact that I'm a master sorcerer doesn't make this any easier. I don't have the luxury of exploiting my power, for it could bring unwanted attention from the Creator, who would foil or interrupt my mission. I must use diplomatic means to gain prominence without using the name of my commander..."

Derideon's name was shrouded in infamy, spoken with contempt and disdain by Harmonologists and most of the population, who viewed him as a nefarious entity, spoken of in whispers behind closed doors. Kragon knew that conquering this new world would take a stellar reputation, which was easier said than done.

Kragon realized that he would have to become president to complete the agenda set out for him by Derideon. After his investigation at the library, he walked the bustling streets of Manhattan, dodging traffic for hours on end, scanning his surroundings in pursuit of any remnants of the numerous minions he had secured before his last departure in 1934. They had been based in the lucrative insurance company storefronts sprawled within the downtown business district.

Kragon's inspection was unsuccessful, so he reevaluated his reconnaissance mission. He determined that his leader's goal was to instruct him about temporal attributes when persuasion was applied by means of force. Kragon halted his futile, mentally exhausting trek near a prominent university located in an affluent part of the city. He checked his outer appearance and saw that his attire was antiquated, conspicuously unflattering compared to the socialites around the campus. Usually, this dilemma didn't occur, as there were typically servants, disciples and informants in position before his arrival, eager to keep him up to date with fashion and current events. Obviously, this support network no longer existed, and he was bereft of the pleasures he had enjoyed on previous excursions above ground.

Kragon relied on the vast amount of information he had collected and retained cerebrally about his virulent opponent, the Creator, who could summon deadly forces in an instant. Consequently, Kragon vowed to circumvent the Creator's wrath by not drawing any attention to himself, while also allowing the book's teachings on Harmonology to reverberate within his mind. Kragon wanted to familiarize himself with this indoctrinated dogma of modern man, to blend in with their philosophical rhetoric. At that exact moment of reflection, he had an epiphany.

Kragon recalled a passage in the book that told of an uprising in the latter part of the twentieth century, in which the Creator and his followers, the last surviving Vindicators and the newly formed Harmonology sect, dismantled and executed the group of loyalists in New York who still worshipped Derideon's name.

Kragon began to understand what had happened to his disciples stationed in hubs and businesses throughout the Wall Street district and the various boroughs of New York. They were gone... wiped from the face of the Earth.

All Kragon's allegiances would have to be reformed and he readied himself to start anew. With a clear and reformulated mind, he began to map out his course of action. He first created a license and a past identity for himself, since he hadn't been aboveground in the better part of a century. Kragon began to change his perception of the mission; it changed from bleak to intriguing, encouraging his confidence and demeanor as he meandered across an Ivy League campus in upstate New York. He weaved through the swarm of students between classes, and headed directly to the admissions building with the intent to enroll.

Upon arriving, he was approached by several fraternity representatives and coaches who were hoping to curry favor with the strapping young man, nearly a thousand years old, but standing tall at six-foot-nine and 270 pounds.

Kragon didn't look a day over twenty-four and the identification card and transcript he had fabricated reflected that image and date of birth, making him a twenty-three-year-old transferring from military to civilian life, with an associate's degree in political science and a minor in psychology from a junior college in Kansas. After registering, he exited the building with a handful of promotional flyers from students and staff members requesting that he join their clubs and sport teams.

His objective was now clear, but there were a few loose ends to tie up, such as financing his tuition and finding a place to live. Other than these particulars, most of his issues had been handled to a manageable degree, allowing him to accelerate his purpose.

Kragon had traveled seven miles by foot past countless mansions and well-manicured lawns, looking for a means of making money in this new world. Kragon entered a mall on the outskirts of the posh residential community, where he finally witnessed a transaction, which enlightened him on the exchange of currency in this new era. People no longer used cash or credit cards, but instead relied on a computer chip inserted in their arm that contained all their available funds, including bank account information, making access to currency efficient and readily available.

Kragon had to perform a bit more sorcery to procure enough currency to survive. Fabricating a past was his first task, but his present and future state of being had to be genuine to outside observers, especially since he aspired to run for public office, with the eventual goal of securing the presidency. Kragon finally made his way to the inner city after walking over fifteen miles from the university, and was approaching the location where he had exited the portal. That was where he decided to lay down roots and rebuild Derideon's empire. While examining the terrain, he noticed a large gathering of picketers outside the local gentlemen's club, on the lower east side of Manhattan.

Kragon entered the establishment to see what the commotion was all about, and to gain insight of the patrons' stability by monitoring their activities. He wanted to see if they could be recruited to his cause. Eventually, he would need to build his forces, depending on the viability of these citizens. If conditions were good after developing an association with those occupants, perhaps he could reorganize them into his new following of converts, which would be instrumental to his success as a future politician.

CHAPTER 13

Kragon entered through the steel front door, which had the image of a provocative woman etched in the reflective one-way glass. There was no bouncer collecting cover charges, so Kragon casually strolled past the stage, heading to the back near an illuminated VIP section adjacent to a wet bar. He sat down at a swanky booth, decorated with LED mood lighting outlining the seating arrangements. From that reclined position, he could scan the club and covertly conjure spells without being seen or disturbed by the strippers and barmaids. The people in attendance and those employed there were considered derelicts of the community, and the crowd outside was protesting to close the doors permanently due to the nature of the establishment. As Kragon sat there eavesdropping on the boisterous commotion taking place in front of the building, a barmaid approached, asking why he was there. His presence seemed suspicious; he hadn't ordered a drink and it had just turned 5pm - much too early to see the good dancers, who wouldn't arrive for hours.

118

Kragon answered her cordially, not wanting to incite anger in a potential recruit. "I'm new to the area, and I needed help finding housing. I also wanted to exchange some precious metal for an under-dermis currency chip." The curvaceous waitress laughed aloud at his response, but tried to compose herself.

The barmaid spoke in a humorous salacious tone. "Handsome, I don't know where you're from, but you aren't lying... there's no way you could've lived around here. I don't mean to laugh, but I've never heard someone ask for a UDC like that. You're sexy as they come, although you're a little outdated with that wife beater and flaming sword medallion... not to mention the khakis." She sneered enticingly, and Kragon was intrigued, wondering what she was going to say next. "You must be from upstate. I haven't seen any men who talk or dress like you around these parts. You've also got outlawed snakeskin hiking boots, and I gotta admit... those look hot on you. You got a name stranger? I can't keep giving you compliments without a name..."

Kragon gave her a lustful grin and handed the voluptuous woman his license. "Your name is Kragon... Thomas? Sweetie, you runnin' from the law or something? That's a mighty strange name. Well, Mr. Thomas, they call me Luscious and you can do the same."

By that point, Kragon was willing and ready to answer any questions from the flirty, overzealous woman. "You heard correctly... as I've stated, I'm not from around here. But I'm going to school just north of here. I need to transfer this gold currency that I'm carrying in my satchel to a UDC. When I attempted to pay my tuition, I was told that coins and paper money are now obsolete. I'm from a farm community in Kansas, where they still barter with tangible money... and handshakes. Hopefully, you and I can work out a similar arrangement. Perhaps you can assist me and I will compensate your efforts."

Luscious was intrigued by Kragon and decided to help him. She was enthralled by his appearance and mannerisms, and this interest didn't go unnoticed. "I will assist you, Kragon Thomas... but the person you really need to meet is my boss,

Gooch. He's downstairs in his office. He can deliver the UDC and everything else you need. Gooch is the man to see. I hope you brought enough cash, Jimmy... that's what I'll call you in the bar. His services don't come cheap, and he'll probably make you work in the club. Jimmy, Gooch always needs protection, and our bouncers have a high turnover rate. The protestors pay them to quit, funded by the Harmonologists. I don't think that's your style though, being bribed by halfhearted incentives. You look like a real bone crusher with a brain to match. I'm impressed, so maybe Gooch will feel the same way."

Luscious descended the steps near the rear wall and crossed through the corridor to summon her boss.

Meanwhile, Kragon began cautiously speaking in *kabar*. He needed to cast an enhancement spell in order to increase his currency, so that he could do business with Gooch. He was distressed because this wasn't a major conjuring, but had to be handled carefully. He didn't want to alert the Creator or the Harmonologists of his presence by using a large power surge, which would leave a signature that could alert someone to his presence.

Even so, Kragon decided to take a chance, knowing that time was running out; he also sensed that there was enough negative energy outside the club to mask his sinister work from being detected. The time was upon him and there wasn't a moment to lose. The air was ripe with dissension and chaos, making it the perfect medium to cast his spell undetected. After finishing his brief splash of sorcery, the satchel he entered with filled up to the brim with 24-karat gold coins. Kragon decided not to reveal the full extent of his assets, so he took out a portion of the valuable coins, totaling roughly three million dollars, placed it on the table in a gilded sack, and waited for his benefactor to arrive.

Kragon strolled to the entrance and peered out the window at the top of the sturdy steel door. He saw that the crowd had doubled and become even more irate, protesting louder by the minute and interrupting pedestrian and vehicle traffic headed to the nightclub. They yelled for the bar to close, stating that it ran counter to the government's agenda for peace and prosperity.

They claimed that the club was perverse, and was unwanted within their community, causing moral decay in the city.

Kragon knew that if the mass of protestors got any bigger, it could alarm the Harmonologists, whose belief were rooted in conformity, not obstruction, to the Creator's will. The demonstrators' motives were evident, and were opposed to Kragon's advancing scheme that he hoped to organize with Luscious and Gooch. Most of the mob outside didn't practice Harmonology, although they were incessantly begging participants to get involved with their cause to close the club.

Kragon realized that he would have to put a stop to their behavior. As he stepped away from the window and walked back to the table, he spotted Luscious standing next to who he assumed was Gooch, a stout, olive-skinned man surrounded by an entourage of Mafioso. One of the men was pushing a cart, which held an ominous surgical tray filled with scalpels, gauze and a laptop.

Gooch spoke matter-of-factly, exhibiting little emotion. "Why have you come here? Are you an informant for the fools outside my door? For your sake, I hope not, as no one has survived trying to infiltrate my organization. I can snap my fingers or make a call and you will be dead. These men beside me are hired guns that my brother Sammy lent me. I'm grateful for the extra muscle, but I need a true skull-smasher to call my own. Is that what you're willing to do for me? Luscious tells me that you're from Upstate New York… you running from the law and looking for a place to hide? If so, you've come to the right place. I can give you what you need to navigate through this Harmonology-regulated, Unitarian government."

Kragon responded with a tone of assurance, but also dominance. "You don't have to practice Harmonology to live within this society. There are two main groups in this country. Those who practice Harmonology and those who believe in science, and what they see to be self-evident through tangible proofs. The practitioners are in bed with the Harmonologists.

Furthermore, it states in the book of Harmonology that they share the same principles, except that one denounces the Creator's existence. Basically, it doesn't make a difference which

121

side you choose; they rely on the conflict with each other to control the public. Luscious calls me Jimmy, and that's fine with me, but my actual name is Kragon Thomas. I thought you might need my legitimate title to program the UDC.

"Gooch, I will answer your questions. I am not a spy, nor do I have any allegiance to those pestilent protesters outside. I have not come here for fellowship or to admire the women on stage. My reason is simple and unassuming. I'm here to make money and protect your nightclub from the mob outside your front door. Therefore, being an enforcer of your domain will be more than acceptable. Your dilemma can also be solved very quickly; I can turn those picketers into advocates of your business, and rebels against the same institution they currently support and protect. My last boss knew the potential I possessed, and never questioned my motives. I understand your concern, but I'm not a threat to your enterprise. I currently plan to attend university, but I come from Kansas. My past has been plagued with violence, and I wish to start over and create a new identity for myself, which is why I need you to install a UDC. When you insert the profile and history, it must be legally unblemished, representing a pristine appearance to the outside world. In exchange, I would enjoy ridding you of those who oppose you. I've come here for the reasons Luscious stated... I believe that you can assist me, and I can do the same for you. Now, let us begin. I have currency, but I don't have time to waste. I need prompt results, Gooch."

Gooch was astounded by Kragon's declaration and confidence. "Jimmy, I'm impressed. I can also provide the service you requested, but it won't be cheap. I need a hundred thousand up front and two hundred thousand after the UDC is installed. You are welcome to stay above the club in one of the apartments I own, rent-free, if you work as a bouncer and bodyguard for me. I need someone reliable, not only strong, but also smart. I have the tools at my disposal to build a lucrative financial empire, and you can share in that wealth. If you don't have the cash right now, I can loan you the money, and you can work it off by doing various odd jobs I require. Luscious, lock the door."

122

Kragon spoke clearly; he had to set Gooch straight and let him know that he wouldn't be bribed or controlled. "I'm not a gun for hire, nor do I need a loan. That sack on the table contains enough gold to pay for the UDC and your rent indefinitely. I want you to put seven hundred thousand on the chip; the rest is the compensation you requested. Time is of the essence. I don't have patience for indecisiveness. The time for action is now; therefore, I am willing and ready to fulfill my purpose. You will benefit from my eventual rise in society, and I can prosper from your unsavory connections to the black market. If you need my help and I am available to assist you, as I am at present, then I will be obliged to do so without hesitation."

After Kragon spoke, Gooch nodded, slightly shocked, and prepared to begin the operation, which was a delicate two-step process. The first step was to pay off the treasury officer, who computed the money to be placed on the chip. Gooch was busy on his laptop, attempting to contact the government official. Once confirmation was established, he would transfer the gold coins to his location. In exchange for the seven hundred thousand in gold currency, the unscrupulous government treasury officer would apply one million to the UDC, leaving him the valuable gold coins to exploit as he saw fit. He would return half the coins to the treasury department vault, recording a smaller value of deposit, while the remaining funds would be embezzled into his bank account. The second step was to insert the UDC into Kragon's forearm. Gooch brought the chip over, which was completely booted, formatted and flashed.

Kragon extended his massive left arm and Gooch injected him with a local anesthetic before making a two-inch incision. He then inserted the device under the dermis, while Luscious began cleaning and placing stitches on the wound. Lastly, the gauze bandage was applied and the procedure was complete.

Gooch had put his fictitious identification, life history and over-embellished finances into the system, now located on the chip in Kragon's forearm. He was officially modernized and able to function in society, without incident or difficulty. He promptly left the club, stalking off the property, past the dispersing crowd. He mowed through them, opening a path of befuddled onlookers who dared not confront the barreling juggernaut, as he made his way to the transport hub to catch a bus to the university.

He took advantage of his cash supply and paid his tuition, completing the registration that had been left undone earlier that day. At the university, Kragon would be able to expand his range of manipulation and increase his knowledge about modern social behavior. He wanted to learn everything relevant to capturing the best souls, as their life forces were crucial to his rise to power, even though most of the energy would be transferred to Derideon for his release from the abyss.

Kragon did not see this as a surrender of power, but rather as an opportunity to enhance their joint endeavor. He was aware of his position, subordinate to his ruler, but Kragon also saw himself as second-in-command within Derideon's diminished kingdom.

A month had passed since he first entered the gentlemen's club. Kragon's academic career was also progressing at an expeditious rate. However, the demonstrators were increasing in numbers outside of Gooch's establishment and it was only a matter of time before Gooch would take Kragon up on his offer to disband them.

He made his way to his apartment as he did every day, pushing through the mob and going up the fire escape ladder at the rear of the building. Kragon unlocked the door, but heard Luscious in the hallway speaking with Gooch as she left her apartment, which was directly across the hall from him. He heard them talking about the protestors, and how they were hampering business. Gooch was telling Luscious how clientele attendance had drastically reduced, and more than half the staff had been let go due to the club's dire straits. Consequently, Gooch explained, Luscious would be working the pole tonight, and the bouncer, one of his other bodyguards, would attend the bar.

Gooch also said that he would personally work the door if Kragon declined. At that precise moment, Kragon pulled a lever on the wall near the back door, retracting the fire escape ladder

124

from the rear alleyway. He walked up the inside staircase after locking the door behind him, heading towards his apartment, a briefcase and books in tow.

He stopped and acknowledged the two of them conversing in the hallway. "I couldn't help but hearing your discussion, and I loathe what is happening to your business. I haven't been ignoring this issue; in fact, I was cautiously considering all my options before reacting. I must be mindful of my public associations and the endeavors I pursue. Nevertheless, I can no longer stand by while this gang of hoodlums menace and aggravate the patrons and employees of your establishment. I overheard your desire for my assistance in the club tonight, and I am at your disposal. If you need me to work the door, I will. Also, I will handle the crowd outside your premises. I have listened to your cries for restitution, and now is the time for deliverance from what you have endured as a result of this oppressive horde. Every day, I come back home from the university and witness fewer customers, yet the surge of protesters is increasing exponentially. However, I was unable to intervene, due to the influx of media that surrounded the dissenters rallying around the building. Today, they will not be as fortunate. There is no press or media coverage today, because President McDarby is visiting city hall, and all available media professionals will be redirected to his position. The window of opportunity has opened, and your opposition will never confront you again."

Gooch was bewildered by Kragon's words. "Jimmy, I don't understand everything you just said, but I gather that you're tired of these bastards harassing me, and now you're ready to kick those picket signs up their asses, right?"

Kragon nodded solemnly, and Gooch smiled wickedly. "Well good… it's been a long time coming. I'm glad that you've decided to get involved. Luscious tells me that you come home and never leave the apartment until heading back to school, so I hope all that Ivy League schooling gives you the strength to get rid of this swarm in front of my property. We're the only strip club left in this state where you're not forced to listen some

Harmonologist or practitioner harp on and on while you're trying to enjoy a beer and watch some ass bounce."

Gooch slapped Luscious' immense bottom after that statement, and she provocatively walked past Kragon, swaying her hips side to side, teasing him seductively. She was wearing a fitted black transparent dress, riding high up on her thighs to reveal a red thong beneath the fabric. She spoke slowly to Kragon, pushing her breasts out, hoping to draw his eye. "Jimmy, this could all be yours if you grab it. I know that you want me, so stop working on them books all day and come work on me, big boy." She dropped a pen on the ground mischievously. Her ample frame bent over to grab the pen, which seemed to mysteriously roll away from her, while repeatedly exposing her breasts and buttocks to Kragon.

He smiled hungrily at Luscious. She was a sight to behold, and Kragon couldn't completely ignore her advances. He was captivated by her aggressive nature and stunning curves, but even so, he knew that the time wasn't right for him to indulge. There was business to handle first, namely involving the elimination of those protesters. He grunted in response to her advances, and moved towards his apartment.

Kragon unlocked and opened his door, looking around his sparsely furnished apartment. He removed his shirt and tie, revealing a form-fitted blue tee shirt, which accentuated his rippling frame. He closed the door behind him and strode down the hallway, following Luscious and Gooch down the steps and into the club. It was nearly five in the afternoon, and the doors were about to open, so Kragon took his position near the front entrance. Gooch and Luscious occupied their designated areas, and the protesting crowd outside began to overrun the sidewalks, agitating potential patrons. Regardless of the protests, some faithful customers managed to push their way through the blockade, entering the club disgruntled and irate.

Kragon greeted and took the twenty-dollar cover charge from the few dozen patrons on their way in. None of them were in the mood for small talk, and voiced their open contempt to Gooch about what had occurred outside the club.

INTRINSIC

One particularly annoyed man spoke for the crowd. "Damn, we come to Gooch's almost every day, but now we're getting harassed on the way in and out. Plenty of people want to come here, but get turned around by that rowdy crowd stalking outside these doors. We've put up with this shit for two years, but it's getting old, and the protests are getting worse. If you don't do something about this, we won't be coming back." Heads nodded around the room, supporting the ultimatum.

Gooch glanced at Kragon and gestured casually towards the door, as though he were suggesting that Kragon spring into action and get rid of the problem right then and there. At that point, Gooch approach the customers with a smile on his face. "I'm grateful for your business after all these years, truly. I hear your concerns, and I'm in the process of handling them. This man, Jimmy, has the expertise and fortitude to wipe out anyone foolish enough to disrupt my club. These demonstrators are a public nuisance to the tenants who occupy this building, and they are destroying this legitimate business. Fortunately, Jimmy is going to put a stop to all of that today. He has assured me that this will be resolved in short order. I will let him explain his position, or answer any questions that you may have concerning security."

At that, Kragon walked towards the customers and addressed them. "Gooch mentioned the dilemmas we have been facing with these hooligans masquerading as protesters. I've witnessed their disruptive actions and behavior firsthand, every single day, just like you. I am ready and willing to put an end to the chaos they've caused here. And you will all bear witness."

127

CHAPTER 14

Kragon approached Gooch and Luscious, who stood near the door, peering out the window at the gathered crowd. They wanted a front-row seat, along with the rest of the patrons, to see justice being served. Kragon exited the club and stalked straight towards the heart of the crowd, confronting them with a fearless, booming voice. "You are gathered here to impede social and economic progress, but who has given you the authority to judge other men? Is there a legislator amongst you? Or are you harassing this establishment without proper judiciary command? I've seen your tactics of pestering patrons and shaming them for coming here. Is that what Harmonology teaches you all to do? I don't think so, or else they would be here beside you. No... a true Harmonologist observes and follows a doctrine of unity, not division, and advocates justice, not inequity.

"You are a headless horde, with an agenda based on destruction. You are nothing more than a group of rogue dissenters, bent on pushing your cult campaign throughout the inner city, crippling businesses in the name of your morality. By that same reasoning, I will punish your group until it withers, and enjoys the same misfortune as it has caused to others. Hundreds of people have lost their jobs due to your fanatical teachings and distortions of Harmonology. Your crusade isn't endorsed by the doctrine's most influential supporter, President McDarby; you are acting alone. I am here to finalize and extinguish your presence in front of this establishment. Disperse or be dispersed; those are your only options."

The antagonist with the megaphone approached Kragon defiantly and began to challenge his orders. "Why should we leave when our job isn't done? My comrades and I have made it our duty to close down these unsavory, unadulterated flesh spectacles in the heart of our city, and we've been tremendously successful. Many have crumbled under our barrage of verbal and financial assaults. Our relentless picketing methods have brought even the best to their knees. We are well within the bounds of the law, so there is nothing you can do to stop us, Sasquatch. Why should my associates or I have any fear of you? Intimidation doesn't work; many have tried and all have failed."

Kragon smirked at the man's claims. "I will be the exception to that success; by my hands and actions, your parasitic little infestation will end."

Without another word, Kragon launched himself at the hefty activist, grabbing him with both arms and catapulting him several feet into the air. The man slammed into the side of a utility pole, where a metal utility box had crushed his spine. Kragon walked over to the man, who was screaming in agony for mercy, and stepped down hard on his neck, crushing his windpipe like an egg. Just as the protester began to teeter into death, Kragon released his massive foot, allowing the victim to inhale just enough air to stay alive.

The remaining picketers were shocked, and stood trembling in terror, hoping their fate wouldn't be the same. Kragon ignored them and strode away from the scene, leaving the man crumpled on the sidewalk in a puddle of his own blood.

As Kragon returned to the entrance of the club, the shattered man's emotionally deflated supporters stood over his wrecked frame, futilely trying to offer assistance and praying that their mortally wounded general would not die.

Gooch, Luscious and the rest of the club's occupants were huddled under the awning near the entrance of the building, cheering with exhilaration. They greeted Kragon with congratulations and claps on the back. He was their savior, messiah and avenger, returning to them without a blemish or scratch. He had silenced the protestors and ensured the trust and respect of his associates. The mayhem outside on the street dissipated as the conquered agitators picked up their critically injured companion and dispersed.

Business in the club picked up throughout the night. Hour by hour, more people entered the door, drinking heavily and tipping Luscious well, who was dancing nearly naked on stage, enticing scores of men to throw tips her way.

The next night, it was even busier, and Gooch had to call in more dancers that had been previously let go in order to accommodate this new influx of customers. Kragon continued to fill in as a bouncer, working the door near the UDC station, where patrons' arms were scanned to verify age and collect their cover charges.

However, throughout most of the night, Kragon's attention was focused on Luscious, who danced and gyrated wildly on stage, sliding up and down the chrome pole, flirting with men and women that tipped her heartily at the UDC station on the side of the stage. By the time she left the stage after two hours of performing, Luscious had earned over two thousand dollars and the house had brought in nearly ten more. Gooch was pleased, to say the least, and eagerly ushered the other dancers onto the stage to the hoots, yelps, and whistles of hungry men and women feasting their eyes on the buffet of flesh. The women bounced and swayed around the room, giving lap dances and extracting funds from willing customers with portable UDC scanners attached to their thighs.

Luscious was done for the night, her wallet filled, so she stopped by to see Kragon on the way to the dressing room. "Hey soldier, I'm about to get wet and lathered up back there, if you want to join me, or protect me, don't hesitate. All the rest

130

of the girls are out on the floor, so it'll just be you and me, Jimmy. Come on, baby... live a little. Let me be your project for the night. I guarantee you won't regret it. Have you ever been with a woman like me? I'm just like my name... luscious. Men and women have left their spouses for the chance to be with me, honey... so if you're up to the challenge, you know where to find me."

Kragon was definitely ready to feel the touch of a woman, as it had been nearly a century since his last time. It was 3 am, the club was closing soon, and the last occupants began to filter out. Gooch expressed his satisfaction with Kragon's excellent work ethic, transferring more currency to his UDC as a tip for the night. Kragon thanked him and headed upstairs, seemingly distracted. He showered and thought about crossing the hall to see Luscious that evening.

He didn't have to wait long or go far, as she was standing at his door when he opened it a few minutes later. "What a coincidence! I just grabbed a pail of ice and some bottles of champagne, and then we intersect like two trains heading straight for each other. I bet we'll make one hell of an explosion when we collide! You ready for that, big guy?"

Kragon was not surprised by Luscious' blunt speech. He knew that she was attracted to his power, wealth and dominance, which was all part of his plan. The more that people admired him, the more influential he would become, making him an even stronger candidate for future ruler of the nation.

He was already planning five steps ahead, and knew that he would have to reinvent Luscious into a woman worthy of being with a president, if he planned to use her as a running mate in his future campaign. First, however, Kragon had to find out if she could be instructed in higher learning and speech, which would be essential as a First Lady.

He knew that this early morning rendezvous wouldn't yield the answers or results he needed, but he could please her, and thus create more intimate relations between them.

Kragon obliged to her lustful demands and allowed her to lead him into her apartment. "I can no longer resist you, but Luscious... are you more than just an instrument for sexual

131

release? Should I invest my time, knowledge and instructions in you? If not, I won't be disappointed, as everyone serves a purpose of some kind, whether large or small, but I wish to know what use you would like to be in my life." She was clearly not expecting such a deep or heavy question, and she was stunned momentarily. Before she could speak, he pushed on.

"I don't know where you fall into the equation of my future, but for now, I am only interested in satisfying your every desire. Let us become one, for the time has come, and we must take advantage of this moment, to unite in carnal ecstasy. Come now, Luscious, let's use this ice before it melts."

Luscious giggled at Kragon's studios verbiage, and matter-of-fact way of expressing himself. She honestly didn't care much about what he said; her only real ambition was to have sex with Kragon, so if it meant listening to his rambling nonsense, she would gladly do it.

They came together multiple times that first night, and every other waking day thereafter. Kragon was accelerating at the university, earning the respect of his professors and colleagues.

Even though he was living an illicit sexual lifestyle with Luscious, he had to maintain a public image of propitious behavior. Kragon walked a thin line; his criminal affiliations couldn't overlap or affect his scholastic achievements.

He slowly began infusing Luscious with knowledge, pushing the limits of what her sex-crazed mind could retain about his political aspirations and understanding, including world affairs. Luscious was becoming more proficient in her oration, which allowed him to extensively expand her canvas of knowledge. The more she learned from Kragon, the more astute she became as a student, gaining valuable attributes and increasing her self-worth.

As months and years rolled by, Kragon became known by many people within the state and beyond as an elite scholar and deft businessman. He opened several cost-efficient organic grocery stores that were utilized by the community, vendors, and surrounding restaurants along the Manhattan and Wall Street business districts.

Four years had passed since Kragon first stepped back on Earth's terrain, and he was now enrolled in graduate school, pursuing a law degree. Kragon had gradually separated himself from working at Gooch's nightclub and his shady dealings, along with any deviant associations that could tarnish his advancing political career. He had made Gooch a great deal of money, and there was no ill will between them.

He still kept Luscious in his life, for she remained beneficial as a future wife and confidante. Kragon was beginning to develop a political track record that would catapult him to the top echelon of his constituents whenever he was elected to public office. He was meticulous and premeditated in his actions, knowing the value of patience. Kragon continued to view his life as a puzzle and was deliberately careful when making calculated decisions, ensuring that his laborious efforts yielded great success.

He thought of his decisions as pieces of a jigsaw, so there was no room for error in his methods of operation. Kragon had many things to consider regarding Luscious, whom he suspected was falling in love with him. She frequently requested stronger, more long-term emotional unity, particularly after finding out that she was four weeks pregnant with their child.

This was immediately identified as a potential problem for Kragon, who didn't need any controversy this early in his career. He brought this matter to his lover's attention. "Luscious, we have been together for nearly four years now, engaging in a non-marital sexual relationship. How we proceed from this point will define our future legacy. I believe that everything happens for a reason, either seen or unseen. This will be difficult to hear, but you must not be seen with me until I run for president. Then, I want you to be my stunning wife, but that can't happen at this immediate juncture. There is still some refinement left and reconstruction needed to improve your public image. I can't allow anything or anyone to hinder my progression into the political realm.

"I've decide to run for councilman of this ward in the fall, so our relationship has to be as inconspicuous as possible, if we want this to continue. I am here on a crucial mission, and triumph is the only thing that matters. Everything I do must be with that intention."

Luscious had some idea of Kragon's ambitious plans for his future political agenda, but was unsure of his intentions concerning their unborn child. This made her uneasy, so she questioned his deeper feelings towards their child. "Jimmy, we've had plenty of discussions about your future political life, but I know very little about your past. You've refined and reformed me into a woman of class and grace, and I will forever be indebted to you. However, not knowing your intentions regarding the baby growing in my womb is worrying. I know that your mind always works miles ahead of others, but I just need a bit of solace and certainty to be whole again. I don't know if you want to be in your child's life or if you even want me to have this baby. Those unaddressed questions are troubling me...deeply."

Kragon was astonished by her composure and ability to be rational in such a stressful, tumultuous situation. He was told by Derideon that his rise would be legendary, and that every deed he performed would catapult him closer to greatness. Kragon also knew that this baby was irreplaceable, for it would have his genes, an extraordinary blend of infinite potential and power.

As he pondered over his contributions and role in the baby's welfare, he swiftly reached a solution. He knew that his child would be gifted, just as he was. However, there was nothing more appealing to Kragon than earning his master's approval, which could be obtained through his accomplishments here on Earth. That was his sole intention at present, but not his ultimate goal. Kragon wanted to become an icon, representing everlasting prominence as a kingdom savior, and a mighty deliverer of retribution.

He wanted his seed to carry on his name and pedigree into the future millennia, by enriching its life as a high-ranking officer in Derideon's kingdom. Kragon and his child would have a huge amount of influence with unlimited privilege, ruling as powerful entities possessing unbelievable abilities.

Kragon attempted to calm Luscious with assuring words of support for the baby's meaningful and undeniable valuable life.

"I care greatly for you and our baby, so ease your mind. I am here for the both of you. It is wise to question all things that worry you, including uncertainties pertaining to any subject or issue. I know that you are concerned about my range of involvement and dedication as a family man. For now, I encourage you to be patient. We have months to go before we make the choice of whether to raise the baby or give it up for adoption. You may wonder whether this matter will cause me to falter or lose perspective on things that are important to my rise. I value our connection, and hope that we maintain it even through turbulent circumstances. We have both been challenged socially and economically, only to persevere, rising to the occasions and prevailing. I proudly reformed you from a pole-dancing barmaid into a wise woman of significant intellectual prowess."

Luscious' tension began to subside at Kragon's word. She wanted to please her mentor and provider at all costs, but not through the sacrifice of her unborn child. Kragon could sense the unhealthy maternal fear and paranoia that Luscious was developing for the baby's welfare.

Reading the situation wisely, he decided to wait on the discussion of how it would be better to let the baby grow up in a more suitable environment, at least until he was a bit older. Kragon had nearly finished law school when she told him of their pregnancy, but all of it had to be concealed. A child out of wedlock wouldn't be compatible with his pristine reputation.

Luscious knew that Kragon's tolerance for this expansive inquisition had run its course. She was observantly aware of his rage, and didn't want to be on the receiving end of his vexations. Although, she had been with many men previously never had she encountered a man of his stature and mental caliber. Therefore, she was more accepting of his irregularities and peculiar mishaps of character traits, that were unaccustomed to her. Luscious struggled to gain some minute sense of control in this male dominated union which failed to be equalized, no matter how she coaxed and persuade his bloated ego. Kragon held true to his principles and was unflappable with his decisions, regardless of what the subject of discussion happen

135

to be; nevertheless when it came to actions of pursuance they usually operated on one accord. At the very least he would listen to her, but when Kragon made an aspiration a goal or an ambition there would be no halting him.

Ultimately Luscious usually got her way and decided to go shopping on Kragon's credit in the posh mall connected to his housing complex he now resided before heading home and leave Kragon' to his own devices. Months accelerated and the two of them eventually made amends toward their continuing relationship for the sake of their baby, and to salvage precious time invested working on their governmental plans of being a crucial component of the political arena. He decided to forfeit his pursuance and elected position as councilman of his local ward to ascertain a loftier more esteemed cabinet position within the locality of Manhattan. Kragon's next position of pursuit was to become mayor.

He thought tirelessly of this ambition while flexing and strengthening himself within his home gym rehashing his goal difficulties and obtainable qualities of the office he wished to occupy. This was becoming an arduous task in recent times, trying to accomplish graduate school and hold public office but it was well worth the commitment Kragon's set records within the state, accomplishing the title of councilman before finishing his graduate degree. The reasoning behind his current tribulations were recurring voices he kept hearing in his head on a daily basis. This steady incoherent transmittance began to disturb Kragon's normal activities and his hopes for running and campaigning for public office. He wondered was this cerebral interference a result of Derideon attempting to contact him telepathically. It had been nearly five years since he left his leaders confinement, so it was in reason that he may be emitting sound frequency to gain Kragon's attention in hopes of verifying the solidification of the mission and progress thus far. The last telepathic connection between them was three years ago, that last all of two minutes before the link was severed, in which Derideon mention in a fading voice the pertinacity of acquiring new recruits, before the utterance ended.

As he stepped out of the shower relaxing himself from an exhaustive work out, there was only one thing on his mind, procuring a dialogue with Derideon. It was of immediate importance for Kragon, so he devised a plan to use the smallest assertion of his life force to remain unnoticed, for the purpose of regaining an incognito telepathic union with his leader.

The last attempt didn't fair too well due, largely to the absence of a conductive symbiotic medium. Kragon chose to use a mirror to obtain this conversion of energy into a state of physical being, to consummate a longer duration of verbal transmission through the two opposite and both contingently parallel dimensions. He dried off and got dressed putting his previous plans for that day on retainer to attend this most pressing concern. Kragon began to speak in kabar using a low barely audible tone, summoning a telepathic link to Derideon. This procedure was a timely affair taking hours to achieve.

The signal and sorcery used to accomplish a connection was inferior in strength to reduce energy emission and traces of power surges to the outer atmosphere. Kragon's spoke this language of supreme divulgence for hours on end until results were finally achieved.

The voice inside his psyche became distinct and recognizable for he could discern every word that Derideon preached in a deep resounding voice. "Kragon, I am in need of viable human converts to procure more demon knights in wake of my accent. I would hope your stint on earth has been profitable to this end and a personification of excellence in achievements. You are here to quantify my arrival, now is the era to substantiate your illustrious work and meticulous effort. Although I haven't been here with you physically doesn't mean I am not aware of some of your activities. If the frequency is right I can read your inner thoughts through telepathy. I could sense confusion and uncertainty of some recent discovery that has taken place in your life.

Notwithstanding, my immediate concern is the preparation that is need to defeat and victor my opponents, who are yours likewise, or do I need to remind you? I would think not considering your awareness to things pertinent. I only assuage

137

this referendum to make you aware of the urgency and persistent dedication required to emancipate me. There are many things for us to discuss, such as your interaction with mankind, how has it benefited you? Are you profiting from your interaction? I've come privy to you possibly creating life on this planet. I never had the opportunity for things of the nature, my only desire was oppressing humanity and extracting their souls to combat the Creator.

The reality of life is simple to regulate, if you are the source of life and death. You choose who carries your name or legacy, having a blood heir is irrelevant in that situation. Kragon you exemplify my point, although you are not my biological son, the power I wield obtained you from the grips of death now you are in the position to do the same. To create life on this earth is senseless unless it provides a service of gratitude. I have been with many women which have brought me lustful joy, but never have I conceived a child. I couldn't risk collateral damage, therefore, I methodically and purposely avoided inseminating my partners. However, you're not a demigod which makes you more susceptible of succumbing to mortal desires. I have immortality coursing through my veins; therefore, the pleasures and interaction of humans are wanted but not needed. Although, you are godlike through sorcery, and your family's preservation of powerful immortalizing spells, it doesn't diminish the power you contain, since these enhancements are perfect over a generational period, intertwining the attributes acquired into your ancestry. Kragon, I am abreast of your activities to some degree, enlighten me to the particulars so that I may access the initiate of those exertions."

Kragon's was prepared to explain his progress thus far to his unforgiven commander. "Derideon, your approval of my mission means everything to me. I meditate and dwell on increasing the vitality of my pursuit to establish your rise once more. I haven't deviated or prostrated from that sole objective. Regardless of participating in mortal activities such as you say, I am human.

"Although I am otherworldly being, who doesn't suffer from man's frailties and inhibitions, I possess extraordinary abilities as you have witnessed. My supernatural gifts, including unfathomable powers, which I use fully to our objective. I had to be acquitted; and in addition, I emerged from a dormant state. I must admit it seems quite impressive in my surmise of events.

"Derideon, your conjecture on my current status of results derived is warranted, nonetheless I am persistently committed to this aspiration you've given to me. Many obstacles were presented at the precipice of my mission that were circumvented with diligence and cunning delivery.

"I am here at your direction and order, to carry out and deliver your agenda with pertinence and zeal any distraction that alters my resiliency or determination is rooted out and becomes null and void to my direction of pursuit. I have established many alliances since my arrival and many more are being created. I have been intimate with a woman, as you may well know, and have created a son through our union, whom I plan to indoctrinate into your army. I'm working every day to situate and expedite the cause in front of me. My son will be an indispensable warrior with the caveat he must have my energy. The mother has also been conformed slightly to adhere to my needs for legitimacy as a public figure with a healthy, social and homogeneous normal lifestyle of the surrounding citizens blending in with society. There are many things you have probably speculated about in relation to my advances on the surface, know this every action I've assessed through scholastic ventures is all relative to our conquest." Derideon chimed in with a derisive recourse. "You are in default of tangible results at this present juncture, concerning the institution of warriors who are a pertinent and valuable requirement in the installation of the empire that will eventually bolstered in this realm.

"I can give you accolades about your mode of operation, nevertheless, I am consulting with you to provide notice of your inadequate service so far in our quest. The bare minimum will not suffice in such a conquest as demanded by my necessity. If you set out a standard to be the best as a general and second in command of a kingdom, only the best effort is accepted by your chieftain. Regardless of your own inclinations of success, it means absolutely nothing until substantial outgrowth and exertion is acquired, and I officiate those deeds you perform. You must create soldiers to accommodate your diplomatic ruse in the event it no longer has an effect or purpose. Even in this world you now live in, non-confrontational and debased of aggression, there are still pockets of resistance and non-conformism that exist, and locating them is the challenge that must be pursued. My advisory message must be received with acknowledgement of your negligent continuation of events in relation to the goal at hand. I'm waiting to see and announce the excellence of your labor, tell me what you plan to do that will exemplify any results that are in action now to ease my tension.

Kragon thought for a brief second before responding to the contrition presented before him. "Derideon I know there are stipulations to my progress or lack of you deem crucial and necessary to accomplishing your aim. I haven't faltered on those amendments nor do I plan to renege on any issue related to enhancing our gain within the workings of this environment that I have been methodically weaving through undetected by the Harmonologist and practitioners, who would both adamantly oppose to the arrangement we have. Furthermore, I can account for all my actions thus far on the ground I currently stand. You enlisted me to particular instruction which I have actively engaged in up to this present time.

"Therefore, I will continue with the agenda set in place under your authority, as long as you have need of my services and expertise. In attempt to accentuate and answer your request about confounding issues you mentioned in regards to me formulating a base of soldiers to convert into demon knights, is a matter I am only slightly regretful for, as it wasn't advertently done, rather a matter of lacking to initiate a specific punctuated date to administer or organize a vast staunch deadly disbursement of foot soldiers driven for the purpose appropriated.

"The challenge and responsibility enacted upon me spikes my internal, irrefutable need to be within our principal elements of war, strife, and soul consumption. This crucial need is welcomed and desired, triggering me back into a familiar state of mind. I will rely on cemented links formed through legitimate

140

and seedy organizations, throughout my current duration they will become valuable components in locating and organizing new recruits.

"The process is underway, and now I must reconsider my path I once sought after. I must ask to be reelected as councilman of my ward, a mayor's job is much to refined for what is about to take place.

"A concerned councilman has a more vital role and a closer relationship with the citizens, a quality and responsibility that couldn't be ignored, but must be embraced as a lure to candidates for soul conversion, a process for utilizable energy and spell abatement properties.

"All these immediate and dire propositions constituted to my attention may weigh heavy on you, Derideon. I am here to serve a purpose of great significance and major consequences as your chief enforcer and demon knight commander failure is detestable conclusion for me, I only know victory. One call to my constituents or affluent proprietors and I am reseated to my previous position, no matter the difficulties or ease of the criteria demanded, I always prepare for alternate situations to arise in my midst.

"I want to ease your mental anguish with the reality of the momentous and gigantic obligation entrust upon my care and determination to exact this conglomerate of cadaverous foot soldiers that shall be banded with speed and diligence. My every motive of operation presently is resurrecting our troops to enhance our invasion, therefore if diplomacy fails blunt fatal force can sway the tide and intensify persuasion."

CHAPTER 15

"Derideon, I speak to you not to make concession for negated duties not materialized; nevertheless, my motive is a truth finding rendition to nullify unproductivity and maximize efficiency elevating a hierarchy of forthrightness in my daily activities. There isn't much I wouldn't do in the name of my emperor to mitigate his approval, although results will correct all deficiency, from this day forward I pledge to be more thorough with executive orders you passed down to me. My intentions were true but that doesn't correlate execution of a directive set in place. I have learned from my negligence and staunchly I am ready to engage upon my task."

Derideon showed little encouragement or reprisal for any of Kragon's initiatives he exhibited and brought forth, so far on his current stint above ground. He spoke to Kragon in a reprimanding way of articulation. "Kragon, I am not conversing with you for your chance to seek praise for necessary actions to enact a directive that you were commanded to achieve, rather I contacted you to direct your focus on discrepancy I have noticed which are going uncontested. The notion of you exerting all your energy to our cause is absurd.

If you had diverted everything you had physically and mentally to doing my will in entirety this conversation would have never happen, concerning a dialogue of mediocre renderings done by you on my behalf. I implore you to be extraordinary on all matters rather extravagant or diminutive, we are up against forces that are gargantuan in totality, allowing only a slight fraction of negligence to be accepted in any of your travails attempted. I only recognized and acknowledge exemplary feats those who serve me and you won't be an exception to this clause. If you want to satisfy my hunger and restlessness, then procure and increase your duly sworn contrivances, I'm waiting to witness your ingenuity and stellar potential that hasn't manifested to my satisfaction, an exceptional delivery of rewards. The honoring of one's deeds are earned and not given, when you perform to the specifications that are promoted by your leader then you will be in contention for my accolades and approval.

"Never depend on others to assist you faithfully on this earth, you know the inconsistency of man and how they can be easily persuaded to lose loyalty and motivation without constant monitoring and persistent pressure related to the agenda assigned. I forewarned you about this reference of trust and allocating prominent responsibilities on your newly acquired associates, for the quickening of deceit and envy will cause many men to stray. Every acquisition made must be done cautiously.

"When recanting spells, it must be done within the lowest depth possible at this juncture. You've learned man's ideology and political system while developing relations and institutionalizing yourself within its political structure those are all indicative qualities that can be lamented. The child you bring into creation is pivotal key to this conundrum, it can be a devastating weapon to our kingdom, or a redemptive annihilator for the Creator, and his soldiers at arms who are known as the vindicators.

"You have initiated a cataclysm of events that are about to evolve into realization. What has occurred cannot be undone,

143

only you can wield stability in this potentially turbulent future to come. I can't hold your hand through the storm and guide you to safety or assist you in completion of the assignment. I can't foresee all happenings either, nor can I prevent you from making poor decisions. Ultimately Kragon's you hold the principal power to your destiny I am only here as of now to instruct you on what I know through preconceived knowledge and prophetic mutterings that have been told by sages for eons.

"The Harmonologists are the modern-day representation of wise orators who control the masses with founded observational knowledge and resources which have all but dried up since 1938, the last time the remaining vindicators were around and alive to corroborate and defend them was in the uprising in Manhattan and the Wall Street business district, which eliminated my disciples established by your ingenious effort.

"This shouldn't discourage you but rather ignite a fire in your bosom electrifying your momentum to assemble a larger force to combat their attacks.

A large assemblage of the previous recruits was formulated into demon knights and the remaining gathering were used for ambassadors to teach my discipline, fueling our life force, primarily mine; nevertheless, a healthy portion of energy was diverged by you and absorbed, enabling the procession of excellence you've portrayed in your academic and professional life.

"I hold no ill will due to your ambitious and self-indulgent ways, however, if the outcome is in my favor." Kragon was in a state deliberate calm to lessen the amount of brain activity that wasn't related ongoing discussion. He wasn't enthused about the mental probe he was receiving, and mad a cognitive notion of ending the loquacious addendum. "I am forever reminded of my inadequate enterprise, that has area which is faltering in some respects. The knowledge gained and Intel received by you only magnifies my momentum to exceed expectations and sure up what is needed. This course of procurement should begin swiftly with regulated development and precise recruitment of militiamen.

144

"I will use all my sources to amass a sizeable unit through exhaustive footwork with laborious hours protracting my every day until a solution is found.

"Make no mistake this is of utmost importance to me, there shall be no compromise from this order given by my father and lord, Derideon, your respect means a lot to the overall schematics of my mentality and how I gauge my accomplishments. Let me engage myself into the logistics of this campaign since there is much work to be done. I haven't a minute to spare with trivial idlings that overtake the mind with doubt and procrastination which only hinders productive activity. The time is now let us proceed.

"Kragon, your word has become your bond and assurance of fidelity towards the reconstruction of my infrastructure and kingdom upon the terrarium realm. We both have spoken that which is relevant to one another, therefore, go my faithfully sentential and do what you must to obtain supremacy, for the hour will arrive where you must prove all things. I leave you with these parting words, never cease with your search for wisdom which intensifies your performance, giving you the highest possibility of perfection."

As those last words were delivered by Derideon, the telepathic connection began to fade, and Kragon step away from the echoing bedroom mirror sending out its last distorted utterance. He leaped into movement arranging his wardrobe and finding a casual outfit to wear to City Hall one of many stop he planned to make tomorrow morning. It would be a day of meaningful exploits where his skills and knowledge would be put under severe scrutiny, by all he would approach to meet his criteria and demands to satisfy the objective of world conquest.

After organizing his attire, he decided to come up with strategy that would help unify his affairs business wise and scholastic into one functioning unit with the aim of creating a swathe of soldiers and army to serve his cause.

He scanned over legal documents and term papers that had to be turned in for class the next day. Kragon would graduating law school by the end of year and wanted to be prepared for the bar exam. That goal would take a back seat to his current ambition. He knew what his ultimate purpose was and nothing could supersede what was order by his Chieftain. This affirmation coursed through his mind as he plotted out his next assessment of reliable options, hoping to implement a collage of suitable aids who could give him leverage in an era where people avoid opposition to lawful commands of governmental rule. It was almost midnight when he decided to retire for the night with many contemplations to attend him through a stressful sleep.

Kragon was awoken by an alarm clock activating within his cell phone on top the night stand. He sprung up from his bed and then step in the bathroom then left out after exiting was on his way, there were many things to attend to.

On the way out of his condo he scheduled an appointment with the deputy director of public affairs at city hall whose job entitles registering and swearing new cabinet members to public office along with human resource and public liaison duties such as addressing domestic complaints and concerns from a lengthy list of citizens that were forward to his office. Mr. Preston was not known to overturn ratified or signed off cabinet position either voluntary or being vetoed out of office.

The very same person Kragon would petition for a cancellation of his previous and a reassignment of his previous councilman position. On the drive to meet deputy director on his hybrid trike he took cerebral notes about how he would persuade the deputy director of public affairs as he weaved through the congested traffic pulling into his reserved parking lane at city hall. Kragon entered the front of the building proceeding through security checks where guards required all non-officials and citizens to have a body and cerebral scans to determine weapons threats and those who may have a propensity to violence and disruptive tendencies by examining electrical spikes in synapses around regions of the hypothalamus.

After the intrusive exam, he started to become familiarized with the procedure he had once not endured since holding public office for the last three years.

Kragon walked down the gleaming marble causeway navigating around elaborate stone columns until reaching the elevator, which he rode to the 20th floor where Mr. Preston's office resided. He was escorted by the department's secretary to the director's office, where he was engaged in a meeting by way of video conference, where a briefing by the mayor who was briefing him on public relation matters and fiscal issues as Kragon entered the room.

Preston decided to wrap up the engaging conversation with mayor Bloodstone in lieu of Kragon's unexpected earlier arrival. He decided to reconvene with the mayor at a later juncture that day, since Kragon was already there for the hasty scheduled appointment. The director pushed a button on his handheld remote retracting the 70-inch LED projector screen mounted overhead back into the wall paneling and then motioned for his appointed guest to be seated in front of his sprawling desk with legal jargon and city zoning blueprints neatly placed.

Kragon obliged and the conversation started to commence with the Preston taking the reins.

"Kragon, I hope all is well, so what's on troubling you? whatever I can do to help let me know. It would be only a matter of paying it forward considering all the opportunities you've provided ward 8 and Manhattan since your tenure as councilman. I am esteemed to congratulate you for the service you provided to our communities.

"Preston, I am grateful for your acknowledgement and gratitude for my service, as you know the affordable organic food markets I established through my district benefits all, restricting no one from the ordinary citizens to our elites.

"Additionally, 20% of sales on merchandise is allocated to outreach programs to dissenters and cerebral rehabilitation internment camps situated on the outskirts of the city. I won't waste your time filibustering; I would like to be reinstated as councilman of ward 8. The decision I made to resign last week is a decision I regret. It was done to organize a campaign to run for mayor this fall. I've come to the self-realization it's more advantageous for my resume, last two semesters of law school, and the citizens of Manhattan for me to continue my previous duties.

"I am aware if granted the position again, that my job will have new amendments such as being a counselor and advocate at the camps. These new complexities as councilman are welcomed and will be instrumental to keeping a transparent relationship with the people of our city that are law abiding and non-law abiding alike, which will be helpful in closing the gap on organized crime by staying aware of the activities of rebellion that are ensuing within these correction facilities." The director of public affairs paused for a brief respite to consider the request and then responded.

"Kragon, I'm at the liberty of repositioning you back to your former office, although, I would need your commitment to be enduring.

"You left your post to seek a higher office and that's ambitious; yet, the challenges of this new pursuit have minimum job difficulties that you thrive on for self-satisfaction which has become indicative of your trademark. I can allow the transition you desire from civilian to public servant and state office holder, if the duration coincides with your intentions of service as our reinstated councilman, that I will document as councilman Kragon Thomas has returned from his leave of absence to his sworn duties with the adage of the new responsibility pertaining to amendments required. If you are in agreement with the discussed qualifications of service, then the seat is returned to your discretion as if you never left it." Kragon's was pleased to know that his chances were visceral and right at the breach of completion so he didn't hesitate to the terms explained by Preston.

"Preston, I am in compliance with all duties of office, and addendums that have recently been inserted as a councilman's itinerary. I will be back onboard as performing public servant as offered from this day forward. I plan to commit and serve a protracted duration of service to my elected seat. Tell Mayor Bloodstone I wish him godspeed on his upcoming re-election, which most likely he will win.

"Also, the new stipulations his office push through for my office is appreciated. I've asked the city council members many times to be more involved with the people, it's good to know someone was listening to my petitions. I know you have busy schedule such touché, until I see you again take care and thank you for your consideration."

Kragon exited the office taking the elevator down to the first floor. After departing the transportation hub he walked through the rotunda leaving the main entrance. He felt enthused as swaggered to his trike and pulled out the parking lot, on his way to his next destination, which was the law school he attended. The plan to resurrect an army for Derideon had many variables each step had intricate role in the organization and formation of this tactical force he would develop. The student center on campus had a debate group taking place in an hour.

He strategized that this could be an opportune event to convert students that wanted to oppose the current system of government to his agenda. Kragon knew that a lot of disgruntled student that attended were loners and underachievers the perfect candidates to be manipulated in his mind and train of thought.

He need a platform to entice and pursue the misguided gathering to follow a new doctrine. The forum had to do with the state apprehending nonconformist and eventually placing them in internment camps when they continued to rebel against the governing system. As he pulled up to the institution a group of lobbyist mainly the debate group were outside the student center passing out literature that objected to the rehabilitation internment camps stating it was just a hoax to disguise a ploy that these facilities were a really permanent institution that you never made it out once admitted.

He walked upon the gathering, reading the pamphlet handed to him, refreshing his understanding on their concerns to better blend into a similar psyche the majority perpetuated within their organization and hierarchy. The doorway was congested with jocks and star athletes who were on the verge of losing their scholarship due to the stringent grade requirements recently instituted for next year, and were hoping their concerns would

149

be addressed. These loud door jammers recognized Kragon from a distance approaching and made room for the councilman and a procession of students following behind him to enter. As he took a seat the speaker of the event was at the podium ready to begin his discussion. At that very instance a rumbustious woman raised her hand interrupting the meeting, speaking out against the legitimacy of the group's intent.

"Hi, my name is Olivia. I am here representing the Harmonologist of your local sect, we believe these forum is going to lead to nothing but instability and rebellion within the inhabitants of this highly acclaimed university. I implore you disassemble and stop agitating rebellion it will profit nothing but insurrections, which your fraternity must take responsibility for, along with the consequences resulting from this caustic allegiance dissolution by the state. Don't let me hinder your purpose of festering contrite workings against order and fluent functionality with lawful citizens who obey their constitutional obligations, these persistent infractions that your group is maturating against authority and the state can't be and will not be ignored without some type of substantial recourse.

"By all means continue your rampage of disparate remarks on the institutions created by intellectual people whose passion is to keep order and tranquility within society. So please don't stop your delusional anarchist rant on my account, you and your associates have been forewarned of the penalties of inciting and organizing dissention."

The speaker was trembling after hearing the ominous words of the Harmonologist which was accompanied by practitioners also who sequestered an explanation of their intent.

Kragon was even more adamant about his decision to convert new followers through his newly appointed position as chancellor converged with added duties as resident counselor to all occupants who reside and are sentenced to long term confinement at the facility. The practitioner was the the next person to speak without invitation. He called himself Maddox who was a chemical engineer at industrial technology company contracted by the government to advance energy sources and become self-reliant reduces the emissions of fossil fuels.

Maddox was enthused to tell the crowd about his relevance to society. He told them about a freon he developed which reenergized through circulatory motion through reverse polarity magnetic cylinder. The refrigerant was infused with positive charged nano bites that continued in movement around the cylinders which kept the coolant activated keeping the coolant cold. This unit could be installed to any device such as a refrigerator or freezer, making an electrical motor unnecessary for a self-contained power source.

The practitioner wasn't finished with his braggadocio rant and gave them options to deviate from their criteria of renouncing authority.

"It's apparent to me that the majority of those gathered are here for retaliatory and revolting pursuance, how can you aspire for productive for your nation plotting against it. I am astonished by the disparity of unmotivated students that are uninspired concerning innovation and don't want to make a difference to their nation. The repercussion for your lack of pride for your city and state will expedite those of substantial means to sequester this futile halfwit rebellion. Your complaints hold no validity to the improvement of humanity, failing to gain ground and influence in the political machine that fuels our economy and creates opportunity for all citizens. I abhor complacency and this organization of peons lack of ingenuity, most of you are speeding to your predestined locations which is a monitored behavior reassignment internment camp. At least I can sleep exceptionally well knowing my tax dollars are going to securing my investments and country from the plight you all encourage displacing productivity.

"I support the initiative the government and state has taken to contain this scourge of mentally innocuous anarchists who want nothing other than degradation to reemerge and persist across our reinvigorated country." Ox, the forum speaker who had been at the podium throughout Olivia and Maddox's interruptive vocal invasion finally was allotted the opportunity to speak. "My name is Ortiz but everyone who is affiliated in my life calls me Ox. We welcome all to our weekly debates and forums, we the hopes of voicing concerns and injustices that are evident in our communities and city.

"Olivia and Maddox came here to tell us we are fighting and tumultuous battle against those which are more insightful and sound minded than us. Nevertheless, this has no bearings our debate group, no matter how they berate us and our itinerary we won't compromise. The camps are a violation of our right to express ourselves as free citizens. The state and federal government stance is clear, either we conform or be conformed by way of institutionalization. To outlaw all the religious practice of old is not a just assertion of authority or the judicial use of power. We should have the right to practice whatever religious doctrine that we find suitable to our spiritual needs. Although we want to appeal these restrictions upon us, we are lobbying in an orderly fashion to organize this intend movement to send a petition with signatures to the state legislature. Harmonologists impede our cause by reflecting on their belief of Harmonology, which emphasizes that all religious must have homogeneous footprint not differing or altering in customs or beliefs. It also states they were inspired by the Creators, agents the vindicators to form this practice, justifying their monopolization of spiritual jargons by their claim it halts discriminative, deviant and disruptive confrontation amongst citizens since everyone was on one accord. Therefore, the judicial branch with President McDarby ratified abolishing all other religious customs within the states.

"As with any good dictatorship there must be more than one oppressive party to enact their forceful regulatory penalties and fines upon the average American which our righteous government supports for billions of funds in the form of bribes by wealthy practitioners who funnel this currency directly to corrupted politicians UDC. The practitioners are a whole new enigma who are against everything related to religion and spiritual enlightenment, their only motivation is scientific progress to increase momentary wealth through invention. No one here is against technological improvements if they don't infringe on our human rights of free will which no longer exist in entirety at this present age. I look through the crowd and see

152

people like me who want change and other bigots plotting to silence our just cause.

"However, we will not relent to their demands. I have organized this group of like-minded students and citizens around the city from every walk of life and profession some were empathic to the mission the rest spies working for the city, state and federal government to bring me down to submission and extinguish the movement. If anyone chooses to help please stand up and be recognized, without ridiculing words but rather use unbiased motives to understand our complaints.

"Maybe one of our accomplished law student who is also a councilman for 8 ward where these internment camps are housed will weigh in on our concerns and sojourn for equality instead of state advocated entrapment centers followed by brainwashing tactics infused within these buildings of manipulation. Kragon was compelled by Ox's oration and the way he presented his argument and rebuttal against those who defamed him and his associates. He decided that it would be wise to answer the speaker insinuating comments which brought him directly into the fray.

CHAPTER 16

Kragon stood up and adjusted his tie, then began shutting off his handheld holographic communication device shaped like a traditional cell phone, projected in midair from an electronic bracelet worn around the wrist which allowed you to message, text, or talk.

"Ortiz, as technology increases humanity decreases, my job as a councilman is to equalize this disparity and bring balance within the community. Speculation about my contribution and dedication to my office is transparently obvious. I have the credentials to assert and expose my remarkable track record; even though, it's unnecessary since I'm not here to gloat about what I've done, but to listen to the forums objective and determine if there's logistic and legitimate debate.

"If you seek change of judiciary legalized restrictions, then you must provide an argument that is relevant to the majority of citizens and taxpayers of an expansive region.

"A grass-roots rebellion navigated and orchestrated by anxious unorganized non-informed ruffians who pleaded for reform— that is a minority cause at best, since the sentiments aren't supported or rallied around with profound endorsements by any political or social parties. I could easily call your efforts a mass of renegades bound together by tranny and mutiny. Regardless, of my assumptions I rely on facts not wild theories unlike you Ortiz and your cohorts.

"If you make accusatory statements about what I'm willing to do and my political affiliates make sure you research those you intend to commit defamatory allegations against."

The speaker offered no response to Kragon's statement of condemnation and scolding remarks addressed to him, but diverted to predisposed disparities he believed were inflicted upon him and his allegiance scattered amongst the participants.

As a result of their lack of resolution, Kragon walked across the aisle past the seating arrangement, exiting the auditorium. He confidently strode to his vehicle and mounted the technologically advanced contraption; where upon gaining acceleration, he was abruptly stopped by two undercover agents who alerted his attention, requesting him to his transportation and follow them to a unmarked car situated at the end of the parking lot where the mayor had summoned him.

Kragon was befuddled. Normally, city officials gathered and corresponded quarterly at the referendum meetings which took place at City Hall in the rotunda. He, being the wiser, became intrigued by this abnormality, contemplating on how to benefit from an eminent conversation with a familiarly debated yet equivalized cerebrally self-absorbed bureaucrat.

Kragon headed for the elongated car as the security details motioned for him to approach the rear door and enter. He stepped into the glass-tinted compartment where Bloodstone had a bottle of brandy and two glasses sitting upon a tray between the bench dividing the back seat arrangement. The mayor offered him a drink as his customary way of greeting his affiliates in private articulations. Kragon graciously declined, stating he had business to attend of exceptional precedence. After the formalities, Bloodstone began his rhetoric.

"I'm giving you the reins of a new program that has been instituted through my directive at character reassignment internment camps at location designated locations in your ward. I have been informed by Maddox you're scheduled to meet and establish a position as counselor/chancellor of that institution. I am confident in your ability to accomplish the feat extended to you with the intentions of reforming rebellious, insolent inmates into model citizens.

"The government wants to alleviate insurrection before it takes on a following within the mass population. The resistance as it has formulated is mainly a fringe movement that has recently accelerated its participants.

"When you enter the camp, Mr. Thomas, you will have full access to the prisoners and their records and those prisoners that have the best chance for rehabilitation.

"Do you have any questions for me? I'm giving you this opportunity to enhance your career as a public servant and I know you are the best candidate for the job."

Kragon was relieved this abrupt meeting was nothing more than formalities concerning his new criteria to his amended duties of office and conveyed that sentiment with his response. "Mayor Bloodstone I'm aware of the stipulations and requirements of my office and plan to continue my exemplary service. I am intrigued with this obligation of service that should curb the retaliatory objective of these insurgent groups that are beginning to organize at an expedient rate. I have no query but wish the best with your reelection campaign in the fall, if there's nothing else to inform me of I would like to go on my way."

"Councilman Thomas I thank you for your service and commitment, to we meet again as always take care." The Mayor and his entourage drove Kragon back to his transport where he then exited the vehicle and rode off in the direction to the camp, which was located some distance from his current location.

On the way there, he notified his secretary through his communication device to alert the staff and warden of his impending arrival. He had to make a stop at various checkpoints before entering the institution, and this forewarning of his visit would alleviate the red tape and hassle of scrutiny at the gate.

The closer he got to the secured heavily constrictive encampment, he noticed the impregnable walls and gate that enclosed the building and surrounding area along the route. Kragon pulled up to the guard station, where the officer carrying a facial recognition scanner and armed with a rifle that contained armored piercing self-exploding rounds open the gate ushering him in.

Kragon drove the winding road towards the entrance to the administrative office where he was met by the warden and security detail who began to invite him into the elaborate meeting hall to discuss matters of importance relating to his employment.

"I'm Warden Mackenzie, and I welcome you, Councilman Thomas, to our internment rehabilitation camp, and with your arrival it will eventually be restructured eventually to a character reassignment faculty, giving prisoners a chance to repopulate society if this experimental program is a success. Our existing staff have made attempts to reform these inmates but many are beyond help. The mayor recommends you for this challenge, stating that you were a stern imposing successful political figure that could persuade even the most harden personalities to change and conform.

"You are in my opinion a perfect choice for this job, and my staff. In addition to the records of suitable inmates, I will afford you all information.

"I will take you on a tour of the grounds at a later time. You are welcome to explore on your own. No one here is considered violent – those members were executed by our psychologist years ago.Any inmate who attacks a guard is led out the courtyard to a hail of explosive bullets.

"We are at a crossroads, and can no longer continue our use of lethal force to correct their violent behavior. This practice has been outlawed by the government, therefore it's crucial we find a more humane solution to the rebellious nature of this blight upon society.

"I will have my guards in the meantime escort you to some occupants that are worthy of your expertise, and are more plausible for conversion. Early today, we had a disturbance at

157

the university in upstate New York, and there may be viable inductees that you may be able to convert before they are corrupted by the other inmates. These new arrivals are college students with a propensity to rebel, nevertheless they have a zest for freedom contradictory to what this place offers, which should motivate them to change their radical ideology expediently. "

Shortly after the warden walked away the guards led Kragon to the institution intake pod where the new arrivals were housed until they could be processed through the system. He was given a lengthy rendition of the charges and reasoning allocated for bring the new prisoners to this specific internment camp by the accompanying officers, as he made his way to their destination. They explained to Kragon that these group of inciters had been under surveillance for quite some time under the premise of apprehension if they continued their activities of organizing rebellion, however they had come to an abrupt decision to follow through with predetermined seizure of all members of this insurrection due to facts obtained about their illicit underground gladiator fights. They were hosting these for wager on University grounds, and they were deemed illegal by the Harmonologists. The punishment for any outlawed activity of a violent nature that promoted the dissention of state and government rule was death or lifetime incarceration.

As they continued the procession, it was obvious to Kragon that his new title was a step in the right direction to enhancing his influence. He inwardly focused on how he could influence the stubborn but pliable assemblage he was about to encounter.

The pod was full behind secured glass door, as Kragon scanned the occupants he immediately noticed most from the student center, but then as he had suspected he saw Ortiz looking deflated and contrite at his present circumstance. This proud ringleader was reduced to a fearful, uncertain man along with his followers, who huddled around him in a state of confusion.

The attending officer buzzed Kragon in and gave him an access card for future visits to restricted areas and other

158

confinement units authorized by Warden McKenzie. He spoke to them in a condescending tonnage after the presiding guard introduce Kragon and his agenda.

"To all that are condemned to serve a possible life sentence here, or worse, execution, if you are unfamiliar with me I am Councilman Thomas. Many faces amongst this gathering before me I've seen at previous events talking against the public interest of order and preservation of peace to the consensus of impressionable students, who listen to your rants on public forums. I have been hired to bring stability and unity to the disorder and chaos that has been created by your vigilante methodology. As the rehabilitation counselor and character reassignment officer of this internment camp, every inmate in this room will have a chance to turn back from their turbulent nonsensical aspiration to resist society rule and political organization instilled, to keep harmony and productivity for all citizens. This very day your student forum group held a meeting. I attended, speaking out against the state and federal government's stifling laws, and how they infringed on your civil and social liberties.

"However, Ortiz, or should I call you Ox as your associates have named you, since we will be spending a significant number of hours together over the next couple of weeks along with your crew, trying to reintroduce structure and the conformity to authority back into your psyche…

"Ox, you are the catalyst for change within your constituents who follow you hap hazardously, doing your bidding unknowingly breaking the law with the hopes of making a difference to cause liberation and free will, nevertheless, this lofty goal is never attained through infractions and unlawful behavior. At the meeting on campus you duped your followers to believe rebellion is the answer for political, economic, social now where do you sit? That's right, observe your surroundings you are incarcerated for illegal and unsanctioned war games were wagers are placed and blood is spilled without the state's approval or taxation. Clearly a violation of public safety and the blatant disregard for the statues and laws put in place to eradicate anarchy. This is an act of mutiny carrying a sentence of death or a lifetime of imprisonment. My job is to work with the group of you before your existence is forever altered within this faculty. The population here is made up of hardened criminal and violators of the law such as you all, without the intellectual prowess to change, if you want to see your freedom once more, conformity, obedience, and law abiding actions to your state, in addition to federal government's mandate is crucial.

"My words to you at the student center were null and void to most of you, which is apparent by your confinement within these walls, although now it will be your respite for normalcy, that has been ripped from this assemblage of marauders that are now under my jurisdiction and unwavering control indefinitely.

"The first step is to submit to authority, Ox, there Is no ultimate conform or stay at the camp until you expire, that goes for the lot of you. Think about your decision before you're processed through intake and filtered throughout the population, then you will not be given the opportunity to join this reform program, instructed by me.

"This particular group I stand in front of now have been chosen on an experimental basis, on the premise of your lack of indoctrination and institutionalization prerequisite to qualify for initiation. Other than those specific there is nothing special about the bunch of you insolent idiots, who thrive on nonproductive contrivances leading to disparity and illegal activities. I will help to bring you back into compliance, nevertheless, there is a price nothing is done without reason you must decide which choice is suitable for you. Anyone who participates in the rehabilitation program must contribute back to the community upon their monitored release into my care, and you will learn how to use your passion to create change within the populous instead of indifference and strife. You will volunteer within the community lawfully, assisting noble causes to beautify the inner city near where you are presently restricted to. It would be behoove you to do so.

"I will be here for a couple of hours in my office setting up the criteria and functionality of my newly appointed assignment.

When you are ready to commit, the process of your enlightenment will being under my command."

Kragon left the anxiety-ridden inmates to their own thoughts and devices as he exited the pod. His job to inform them of his position was secured whereas their options were limited, which contemplated within himself, knowing they would soon relent. The thought of his plan coming to actuality and manifesting exhilarated him. He was guided by the escorting guards to a freshly painted wing of the sprawling institution to his office located on the ground level.

This was a perfect place to organize an army for his ruler he mused, as he looked upon the expanse of his environment. It was isolated to the general population and he could easily conduct training camps and complicated sorceries within its depths. The elevator closed with guards in tow leaving Kragon to explore his new workplace. He walked around the massive perimeter inspecting its attributes and memorizing the layout.

There were many advantages to the domain he could utilize. It contained a gym with mats and a boxing ring along with a cage to promote athleticism amongst the staff and officers working at the camp. A new workout facility was built on the upper level also.

As he walked to a room adjacent to the gym there was a desk and LCD projector overhead to conduct seminars and training course to potential recruits, all these amenities satisfied him greatly easing his mind. He envisioned all the souls he could obtain through this new means of conquest he was establishing at the camp. Just as he was in deep reflection announcement was made for his arrival at the intake pod through his holographic communication device. The warden McKenzie stated that the inmates had agreed to the terms and at his convenience he could began their indoctrination. Kragon responded to the warden requesting that the subjects be brought to his office where he could start the conversion process. He informed McKenzie that it would be a lengthy training process to accustom them to a different way of thinking and behaving, and that he would need a level of undisturbed privacy to accomplish this. Kragon told him that some may not survive the

161

course and some could be killed due to act of violence or severe insubordination. The warden assured him that he had his full support and the immunity of the state behind him with daring challenge he was engaging.

Kragon walked to the transport bay as the doors open releasing the herd of accompanied by officer who ushered them to the cage to be corralled unto the counselor was ready to begin his directive. After the officers left Kragon stood before all 300 men focusing his attention on Ox, who was the most defiant of all. This would be defining moment to exercise control to a potential base of warriors in addition to the existing imprisoned inhabitants. He released the gate hinge motioning for Ox to exit and began to speak to the rebel. "You have taken the first step to being free once more by joining character reassignment program but you must be willing to let your past ideologies go and reconfigure the nature of this disgruntled anti-government mentality you have are you capable of moving past your self-righteousness."

Ox paused for a second and began to speak with agitation and contemptuousness. "I am here. These spineless gnats who are confined with me will no longer persevere and fight, my soldiers have given up but I am not so easily persuaded. "I will not convince you my words and instructions are commands either you listen or die. You will be instructed on certain requirements, that are to be performed daily, deviation from that order will give immediate cause for action and correction for that offense.

"There is no compromise or alternative to the rules of this program, the objective of this character modification program is to teach you all obedience and respect for authority. You are under my control and direction your life and future lies in the balance of whatever choice you choose to follow." Ox stood bewildered and defiant. He didn't want to abide by Kragon's rule even though his options were limited, so he decided to go under the guise of conformity to mislead his counselor into believing his intentions were pure and genuine.

The ploy was an ingenious distraction to throw Kragon off kilter and make him secure with Ox's sincerity. Kragon was

162

ready to allow the leader to sign up and become a participant of the course even if his motive was not reassuring in sync with his demands. He told Ox that he must forfeit his alias and use his government name from this day forward when address himself. This was attempt to curve his ambitious and opposing attitude. Ortiz was constantly challenging the status of his circumstance and allowing him to keep even a small semblance of his former self would be detrimental to the progression of reforming these resistant hooligans.

Ortiz hesitantly agreed to all the judgments he had incurred, at that point of his compliance the rest of the inmates were released from the cage and followed suit with their renounce and dejected leader. Kragon was unafraid of the extent of their numbers and confidentiality direct them to the conference room that was equipped with rows of desks. After the mass was situated in the enormous enclosure the entrance was sealed and Kragon began his lesson on persuasive conformity, this teaching relied on the benefit of blending into the system instead of preaching and enacting division. The lecture was interrupted by Ortiz who seemed to speak for the consensus of inmates under Kragon's control.

"We all have agreed to your terms to abide by the law of the land, and extinguish all protesting, but how long will we be confined to this camp? Most of his here have families on the outside who need our support and attention. Let's get on with the procedure we know that total submission is your state and government requirements, what next with this ordeal? Me and my comrades graduate high school we don't need this redundancy of clarification on topics that are constantly rehashed."

Kragon uttered no more, and strolled toward Ortiz ordering him to stand and address him with respect void of insolence. "When you speak to me my title must be stated with the acknowledgement and permission granted for you to inquire, that requirement goes is valid to all prisoners I command. I am Commander Kragon to all of you, and will be summoned per that title. Ortiz, you have only this option to concede to my order, or face the consequences of your indecisiveness."

At that instant, Ortiz initiated a revolt whereby his followers began chanting his unauthorized and banned title Ox repeatedly. Action had to come swiftly from Kragon to keep a balance of authority, and set the precedence for unadulterated obedience from his subjects.

Ortiz rose to his feet while thrusting his desk into Kragon which crumbled and disassembled upon contact against his girth. He pushed the wreckage to the side and started pummeling his assaulter, throwing a series of blows to his upper torso, while slamming his knee into his gut, leaving him wincing in agony. Kragon then uppercut Ortiz with a vicious left hand sending his bottom molars crashing through his upper gum.

Disintegrating his top molars sent a mixture of jagged teeth and blood down the mangled offender's throat. Many occupants rushed to the locked sliding tempered glass door to escape, unable to, they reverted to basic instincts, approaching their predicament as fight or flight, joining in the melee.

Kragon's warrior senses became incensed. He was excited to release his energy and yearning for carnage. This was an uninvited opportunity to reimburse them for their insubordination and rain down hell upon all who would challenge him. Ortiz stumbled backwards falling into the arms of the approaching mob, who asserted their aid with the intent to come to his defense. Kragon relished the mayhem that was unfolding before him, he decided to get more comfortable, loosening his tie, while unbuttoning his shirt disrobing it exposing his bare chest to enjoy the splatter of warm life fluid that would soon expel from his victims. The bloodletting brought he back to days of old, where he had vanquished scores of opponents who resisted his reign and dominance. At this point of the assault he considered not their humanity, his only assertion was to paint the walls red with their essence, dismissing their shrills for mercy. Kragon wanted nothing other than total relenting to his every word of instruction. Ten opposers rushed him after, laying Ortiz upside the glass door where his head slumped between his chest. Disoriented, he fell and curled up into a fetal position.

Kragon wasted no time dispatching more punishment. As they got closer he lunged in their direction, using their bodies as a punching bag, bobbing and weaving exacting devastating punches, hindering other inmates' pursuit. One by one they met a storm of blows, making their efforts pointless, yet they still advanced to a certain defeat.

Out the corner of his eye he glanced at Ortiz, who gained his equilibrium and started fashioning a shank from a piece of paneling along the lower wall. He knew that this man would have to be put to rest, and Kragon decided to inflict his death in a particularly gruesome manner. All those who had charged him were now begging to submit to his every demand without question. The only exception was Ortiz.

CHAPTER 17

Kragon walked passed the cowering men he had thrashed senselessly, typing the code into the keypad to open the door, releasing the horde to the outer brinks of the containment unit they were housed.

Kragon focused, never wavering, as the prisoners filed out of the room. He kept his eyes concentrated on Ortiz, knowing his intention was fatal and his heart was heavy on vengeance, which could not be explained with rational determination.

The last inhabitants hobbled out in a sheepish gait cautious and apprehensive of retaliation. They knew it was a mistake to oppose such a visceral force, who overpowered them with little effort applied, it was as though he was toying with them, beating the life and resistance out of their essence. Kragon waited to leave the room keeping his attention on his nemesis, which had slipped the weapon under his pants leg where it was tucked in his sock resting against the ankle. He let all the stragglers exit, and then he directed them to the open area of the gym.

Thereafter, they were enticed to resume the scrimmage by Kragon, none accepted this request, instead it was more signs of submission and fear in the eyes of these retired, retreating rebels. Kragon knew that many souls would be harvested today he need them to build his impending army. Nevertheless, there was in obstacle in his way, Ortiz, so he questioned him further, since no one else resisted his rank.

"Why do you continue this unfulfilling charade to oppose me, when you will accomplish nothing but death or defeat?"

Ortiz lifted his battered body off the ground and exhaustively explained his motive for his attacks. "Years ago, I was one of the protesters outside of Gooch's, that man you fatally injured was my older brother, I'm here to avenge his death. I have relished this opportunity for the last four years, watching you achieve scholastic achievements, knowing that you were a murder, who claimed to support the people and the community. My men behind me might are waning in heart and dedication, regardless, of their ineptness I've made other arrangements to seal your doom. I recorded you demolishing and breaking the back of my brother to use against you at the right moment.

"The visual recording is kept within through a retina cam that was inserted into my iris at an early age due to a birth defect. If something happens to me and I'm not released from imprisonment, I will make sure the media observes your reckless murderous ways. I made sure that affiliates of mine would have a copy to release. Now that you know what I can do to your name and reputation, the choices are limited for you."

Kragon knew that Ortiz would be a valuable sacrifice and rise to the agenda he attended to display to the rest of the crowd advocating their disposed leaders rise back to prominence. "Ortiz, your belligerent brother received the death that was required and was sought out due to his meddling in the affairs of business, which halted and disrupted the economic fluency of free enterprise.

"You seek revenge with no true plan of recourse! The visual data that you obtained of a nefarious act I committed means nothing to me. I can quell your attempt to transmit these devices at any time. You've done a nonchalant deed to intimidate me, your hasty plan is futile, considering we're in the bowels of a concrete barrier with walls three feet thick and a ceiling with the same dimensions. Furthermore, any outside connection you have would reside in this room, as you well know the state and local government is thoroughly comprehensive when it comes to gathering inciters. The absurdity of trying to blackmail mc is futile! You and your gang, due to callous retaliatory actions, have now signed a death warrant, that I judicially will enact with satisfaction, for you have placed yourselves in this realm of judgement.

"Ortiz, you and this band of fools set out to become martyrs, even so through all your efforts will remain casualties to a lost cause of rebellion, signifying the end of an era concerning social reform through political protest."

Kragon knew that his time with these rogues were almost up, the guards would become shortly to take them back to their cells, so therefore he need to incite a riotous attack. He walked toward Ortiz who initiated his shank-welding attack, preconceived, and fitting seamlessly within the constraints afforded him, legitimizing his agenda. His goal was to neutralize all the previous attackers in the conference room that could defame his name. These men were hell bent on desecrating Kragon–they wouldn't rest unless he was brought down to their level of despair.

Kragon strategized the importance of the dilemma and spoke in kabar, bringing rage upon his assaulters amidst this time of heightened hostility. He replicated a total of ten shanks, which each enemy received that had diverged his commands previously. They ceased to question how the weapons were in their hands, nonetheless, made every assertion to use them, banding together in unison to slash at Kragon, who was engaged in battle with Ortiz.

The remaining prisoners stood by peacefully. These men wanted no part in the execution promised by their soon-to-be commander and unmerciful leader. Kragon had out his well-devised conjuring into motion. He turned on his holographic communication device, which recorded the incident, and then he routed the transmission to all the monitors throughout the faculty. This allowed inmates and staff to witness everything that transpired.

168

The officers had arrived to picked up the inmates but were unable to gain access to the room. They had arrived early because of the altercation, and the glass doors to the unit remained sealed until the scheduled time for their release.

It would be another eight minutes before they would open, giving Kragon enough opportunity to evaporate the souls of his pursuers, expelling their breath and essence into oblivion. He methodically dodged and evaded the slashing and thrusting strikes Ortiz delivered with his lackeys joining in the fray. Kragon intercepted the next series of offenses by launching off the ground from a vertical stance, plowing his knee in the mouth of Ortiz, disengaging his jawbone from the mandible, completely disfiguring his distorted face. His eyes dropped down to witness the displacement of his facial configuration, as the shank he swung was redirected into his forehead with a force of a sledgehammer contacting his cranial cavity. Ortiz fell upon the concrete with a thud, convulsing violently as his battered body hemorrhaged to expiration.

Kragon stepped on the corpse as blood gushed across the sole of his shoes and pants, competing with the existing blood stains on his face and chest. He was camouflaged in streaks of red patterns going in every direction. He continued his rampage with the officers outside the room cheering gleefully, hoping to see more carnage take place.

The next group of hapless degenerates were soon close enough for him to enjoy his death blows, delivered unbiasedly. He began to crush them without regard for human suffering, collapsing the next two attackers. He rushed in their direction, dislodging their shanks, receiving superficial cuts upon his chest and hands, but delivering unrecoverable affliction to these doomed men, stacking body up as he disarmed them sending their weapons through vital arteries, taking their lives with swift resolve.

Eight were left to exact their revenge—they decided to form a coalition with the mob of bystanders standing along the wall trying to gain sympathy and support. However, Kragon would have none of that, retreat wouldn't be a viable option for these cowards, who wished to destabilize their new state appointed commander. He would only be pacified when this band of hoodlums was sequestered and terminated.

A couple of the wall cohorts were convinced to join, but those who did promptly regretted their coercion, as Kragon charged at the recruits, smashing their heads against the wall splattering what remained of an undeveloped brain into the brick, defusing a halfhearted union before it manifested to fester against him.

His HCD beeped, telling him that he had less than five minutes remaining, and the recording was still active. These devices were extremely durable and accurate letting him engage in extreme activities.

More cheering was escalating outside the door as the officers chanted Kragon's name as he demolished the prisoners. The inciters made on last stance forming a defensive circle to ward their destroyer off from terminating their life. He couldn't help but reminisce on past conquests when conquered adversaries had begged and pleaded for their life. Knowing that this was being monitored, Kragon decided to set a precedent for all inmates to receive redemption from this day forward. They would have to audibly chant his name and call him their chief commander and royal savior, giving him the ability to harvest their soul. He would explain and justify the relevance of this pledge to bystanders and public officials as act of total submission to subjugated command. The whole premise of electing him to this new position at the camp, he would make this crucial decision to exemplify his power by torturing these remaining factors into articulating this essence deriving oath sealing their fate forever, binding them to servitude within Derideon's army or for the use of soul harvesting to fuel his life force to escape his tomb. Kragon strolled and swaggered to the disgraced human makeshift circle and spoke to them of the condition to receive leniency and preserve their life on the condition they spoke the oath with sincerity pledging themselves with full dedication to what they were reciting.

Four inciters dropped down before Kragon and immediately pronounced what was told, he could feel their life force coursing within him, invigorating his core, sending a surge of energy to his pineal gland as it traveled throughout his body, strengthening his intended purpose to capture the souls of mankind.

The other half were hesitant, so he decided to make them submit and give their force to Derideon. Kragon knew this would serve a dual purpose, giving his ruler a gesture of industrious compliance to his demands, and resurrect a level of fear, that could identify the intolerable defiance, which would not be accepted under any circumstance. Expedient retaliation was the new order of sanctions for inmates—furthermore, it would be null and void concerning discretionary review, making the judgement most certainly fatal.

Kragon accosted the first reluctant opposer nearest him before he could slash with his weapon, he bent the resistant imbecile's wrist against the range of motion snapping it like a twig, where he then bellowed in excruciating pain dropping the blade, thereafter Kragon retrieved it, staking the crude device into the tormented buffoon, who automatically began to sing like a canary in unification with his stooges, pledging and reciting the oath.

To no avail, their relenting change of heart came too late, and not soon enough all they could receive was a horrendous passing from this life as their soul was consumed by Derideon.

Kragon had already performed an energy transference spell While performing sorcery speaking in kabar early that day. He reached down pulling the shank from his foot, rapidly severing the Achilles tendons of the three men huddled beside him, who chanted the oath in succession, then yelped in blood-curdling audition, collapsing to the ground.

Kragon picked up his first assaulter by the ankles, holding him upside down where he then commenced to jack hammer the top of his head into the concrete floor, excavating the flesh from his scalp, thereafter fragmenting his skull, sending shards of bone matter flying into his partners, who were shrieking and squirming while moaning on the ground. The brain oozed out of his crown as Kragon tossed the carcass to the side. It tumbled to a stop.

The officers let out more cheers they were anxious to partake in the mayhem, the door would open any second now. Kragon grabbed two of the three on the floor slithering about, leaving one to be dispatched by the guards. He grabbed the two of them, pressing his cemented knees into their spine while they remained in a crouching position, then he rested his elbows on the forehead of both executioners, snapping their necks back simultaneously leaving both heads dangling between the center of their shoulder blades like a worm in a hook.

A chirping alarm sounded, signifying the lock deactivation of tempered sliding glass door securing the expansive unit. Kragon jumped into formation, tossing the last sacrificial straggler unto the pathway as officers entered, cocking their assault rifle and armed with explosive rounds that connected with his chest, opening a cavity the size of a Frisbee, launching his organs and entrails against the wall and prisoners standing there leaning on it at the moment of impact. The terrified inmates started to panic, running desperately in all directions, pushing and climbing over each other, and knocking into guards and officers of law who were ready and willing to unleash their killing spree.

Kragon stood beside them as they opened the gates of perdition releasing life forces into the energy realm to be used by the Creator for whatever purpose that fit his fancy. The enforcement officers unleash a barrage of fire power unto the scattering inmates, leaving desecrated bodies in their wake, when the smoke cleared only one hundred prisoners survived, their garments covered in shredded flesh and soaked in blood and brain matter. Kragon was satisfied with his results and scan the room with his HCD to highlight the results of his productive mission.

He also received a message from the warden speaking of a job well done, and he would notify Maddox and Bloodstone of his exceptional accomplishments in restoring order and setting a standard of uncompromising control and authority over the rehabilitating prisoners.

Kragon took this opportunity to respond back with a voicemail letting McKenzie know he was just getting started with more directives he would devise to ensure the stability of the camp, but was thankful his sentiments, and would discuss those projects later that week.

Kragon didn't want to rush the process being that it was his first day as rehabilitation/ character reassignment counselor, as he had a comprehensive plan to modify the minds of all the prisoners, starting with the hundred inmates that survived the apocalyptic slaughtering that took place in his facility. Kragon ordered these inmates, who were on their knees reciting the oath constantly and graveling at their commander's presence, to stand up and begin cleaning the carnage left behind. They were instructed to go in the custodial closet to retrieve cleaning supplies along with a ladder to reach all the bloody tissue and skin splatter stuck to the walls. The floors were matted, with the same predicament as the walls and ceilings. They agreed with gratitude to do everything Kragon instituted and would later become the first loyal soldiers of his newly-evolving army.

The front had been created now all that was need he mediated was for him to indulge upon his deviance.

The camp mortuary staff carted the disfigured bodies away to crematory located at the rear of the camp, after the process was rendered a sealed letter would be sent to the families notify the cause of their death along with the shipment of their ashes in a metallic box. Kragon had finished the last of his formalities with the warden and staff with one last request before he left for the day. He told them to allow the inmates who was cleaning his office and training facility to be introduced to the general population as deterrent and warning to all those who wish to defy his commands. He was confident these men would speak to other about the horrors they encountered and the necessity to obey, and pledge to the oath given.

Kragon was stained with blood as he buttoned his shirt and zipped up his black leather jacket. After exiting the lower level parking garage, his trike had been brought by a jubilant staff member to accommodate his departure.

After passing the front security gate to cheers and accolades, he opened up his vehicle's engine, reviving it, and sped off, defying all traffic laws along the isolated road. Kragon maintained a fast rate of speed even on traveled roads, and he knew that he was supported by all the prestigious government officials of Manhattan. These powerful men and women who supported him were in his pocket.

As he made his way home he lamented on his return to the camp, where he would increase his influence on more inmates the following day with anticipation. He entered his spacious, newly-decorative property. It was a rustic but well-manicured home for a warrior. Kragon was expecting Luscious to come through. He hadn't seen her in over a week. Therefore, he showered and put on a clean outfit to await her arrival.

Luscious finally arrived at his swanky home, and was buzzed in by security, which monitored the surroundings of the complex.

Kragon no longer resided above the club; Gooch had bought him a condo as payment for resurrecting it, which had recently spawned off into a casino with a hotel chain attached. This was all thanks to Kragon's business savvy and ingenuity; he had become an investor in the venture and helped to amass staggering profits.

He also built far more bridges than he burned. Even though he encountered many obstacles, raising a child at that juncture of his life would be an incredibly time-consuming element. He was aware that the child served a much higher purpose than Luscious could understand now, but it still seemed like an impossible responsibility to take on.

Kragon decided not to speak about the baby again until he was ready to reveal his thoughts more concisely. Six months passed, and Luscious' ultrasound revealed that the baby was a boy. Luscious was huge and noticeably pregnant, with a bulbous, protruding stomach and fuller breasts. Kragon decided that it was finally time for him to unveil his plan for their son.

He sat Luscious down to explain his plan. "Our child shall want for nothing, whether he remains with us or is adopted by a loving and capable family. I will take care of him and provide for all his needs and amenities, but his purpose must also be fulfilled. I have divulged a significant portion of the details about my past, including my present aspirations.

"You haven't told me much about yourself that I couldn't deduce. You're a twenty-something woman, raised in a single-family home, who dropped out of high school and started dancing in the local strip club to survive. We all do what we must to advance ourselves; sacrifices are a part of life. Sometimes we must let certain things and people go, for the betterment of the individual. This doesn't mean the future is sealed for that certain thing or person. I hope you comprehend what I'm saying. A wise person would give their cash cow to a thief and get it back later, alive, by any means necessary, rather than selfishly kill the beast to prevent its seizure. No one profits in that scenario. I haven't told you everything about my life, Luscious.

"Furthermore, the purpose of my existence would be unfathomable. I have a boundless journey ahead of me, and you will be a part of that, along with our child. I'm ready to travel this road to success, and all the steps are in line... failure is not an option. Trust me when I tell you this... our baby shall be infamous in this world, and irrefutably powerful, feared by those who would challenge him. He is a prophetic child, one that will be pivotal to my master's ascent, and will guarantee my position beside his throne as the commander of his army. My son will serve with me, as we bring this world to its end, replacing it with a new order of rule.

"Luscious, relax, get something to eat and continue being a good partner and mother to our unborn child. I will handle the rest."

After Kragon's speech, Luscious was still apprehensive about his intentions relating to their son, and demanded more information. She spoke to him roughly, questioning what all of that had truly meant for her and their child.

This interrogation from Luscious was starting to irritate him, who felt that he had already explained enough. Fortunately for Luscious, he was a patient man and decided to share the truth about his life, emphasizing his intentions to eliminate any doubt from her mind.

"Luscious, I am not here to hurt you or my son. My only purpose is to enable my provider's release from his confinement. I have come to your world to release the one whose name is unspoken, before whom mighty commanders of the past have trembled and fallen... Derideon. I am his chief enforcer, a potent liberator and sworn Demon Knight Commander. I am not from this realm. I was sent here to capture the souls of man and break the shackles of my lord. He has given me the blueprint for his freedom, and if I am successful, I will be the most formidable general in the army that will overtake human society.

"I have envisioned my future, becoming a vessel of vindication, and these visions will materialize if I remain focused, fueled by vigorous and tenacious drive. The Harmonologists are not aware of my presence, which must continue. I must remain disguised to evade the watchful eye of their organization. Luscious, I explained myself to you, not to pacify you, but to enhance your understanding and give you the chance to be a part of the greatest moment in history.

"As I moved forward on this mission, my goal was to enrich you, but now you have become suspicious of my motives, questioning my intent and dedication to you. I am an industrious man that does not have time for these insecurities and fears. You are either with me, or you will be forced to take another path. The child will be nurtured and loved; you should never doubt this fact. No matter where he resides, this neophyte will be enhanced with powers and an ancient language. His skills will be nurtured and developed by my own hand."

Luscious' mouth was hanging open, in shock, not having expected such a stream of unbelievable honesty. However, she had seen enough in the past few years to believe that he was otherworldly. She also didn't want to evoke any more frustration or doubt from her mate, so Luscious tried to appease her lover, consenting to his every demand.

She lowered her gaze to the ground. "Please accept my apology, Jimmy, if I offended you in any way. My only reason for questioning you was for the benefit and safety of our baby. I've never given birth before. I am nervous and afraid, Jimmy. I was also worried that you would force me to abort my baby. I hope you will allow me another chance to earn back your trust.

I panicked, but it won't happen again. Let me be a part of this great struggle; I know that I can be of assistance. I believe in you, Jimmy, and I know that our baby will be well taken care of. I was simply wondering about the stability of life for him once he's born."

He lifted a single eyebrow, and she raised her gaze to meet his eyes. He appreciated her confidence, but did not expect to hear what words she had to share next. "I have heard some truly horrible things about Derideon, Jimmy, now you are telling me that you are in allegiance with that megalomaniac. I hope that you're joking, or just trying to get on my nerves. I need time to think about some things… maybe you should too. I'm going home. I'll call you tomorrow."

Kragon didn't contest her departure and instead went into his home gym to work out. Luscious stormed out of his plush condo, her life falling apart in her hands. She felt disgusted by that man, revealing himself to be nothing but a bloodthirsty killer who wished to suck the life out of humanity.

On the way back to her apartment, she noticed an ominous cloud in the distance, as though the weather was bubbling up in the atmosphere, which made the mood of the day even more disturbing for her. To her knowledge, there had been no mention of any storms in the forecast, but the clouds seemed to be darkening and growing, right behind Gooch's expansive new properties, in the same direction as she was driving. She was curious what was going on, but also decided to view the strange occurrence from a safe distance. Pulling over the car and stepping out, the scene unfolding before her was mesmerizing.

A spinning inverted tunnel with wind whipping around its circumference, was creating a blanket of flashing electrical shocks ripping across the landscape, thrashing in a random, scattered pattern. Nightfall had set in, creating a luminous spectacle between the streaks of energy emanating from behind the building. These erratic disturbances lasted for a few more minutes before abruptly ending.

When the smoke dissipated, a stunning figure stood at the heart of the energy field, a tall, strikingly muscled woman, beautiful and bearing a grim expression, covered from head to toe with sophisticated gleaming armaments.

It was Jatara, who was alive and well.

Beside her stood an elderly man wearing a golden fleece across his shoulders, attentively scanning the area. it was Jonas, apparently revived and ready for war. Jatara and Jonas had been gone for over a millennium.

Luscious stood, awestruck by what she was seeing, knowing that something incredible was occurring, and realizing that she might be right in the middle of it. Jatara, the heroine of so many ancient stories, and Jonas, an epic warrior from the past, appearing on the same day that Derideon's right-hand servant had made his presence known to her?

Luscious didn't believe in coincidences. Something in her gut told her that she and Jimmy weren't done... not by a long shot.

ABOUT THE AUTHOR

Jerry Collins is an industrial furnace operator from Ohio, who loves to drive muscle cars, and has a passion for writing mysterious, thought-provoking novels. *Intrinsic* is the first in an epic series.

www.authorjerrycollins.com